A Thin Line Between Sex and Lies

A Novella

Written by D. D. Miles

Dedications

I dedicate this body of work to my sister-in-love, Jessica Gary-Williams. I love you to the moon and back. I thank God for you!

Acknowledgments

First giving all honor and glory to God, I'd like to thank my husband, Bernard for all of his love and support. To mother, Janice Williams for her loving support. It's not every day that you have an avid reader, who so happens to be a retired Language Arts teacher, at your disposal. So if my subjects and verbs do not agree, or perhaps you come across some misspelled words, blame her. I'm just kidding, but thank you, mommy, for everything. You are priceless. To my dad, Larry Gosha, who is my cheerleader. I thank you, dad, for everything as well; your encouragement matters greatly. Thank you to my family and friends for your support as well. As you can see, I can't take full credit for any of this. I am so grateful to those who have come into my life to inspire and motivate me.

To the Reader: I thank you for taking out the time to read this novella series. Hang on to your hats, wigs, and everything else in between.

Let the drama continue...

Chapter 1

TAMARA

All I can remember is someone saying, "I know just cause...," then blackness. When I opened my eyes, I saw Erica hovering over me, calling my name. She had fright and tears in her eyes. I turned my head to search for Ben. He was standing face-to-face with her. She screamed and hit him, "How could you do this to me? What have I done to deserve this?" She looked like a woman possessed, wearing this black tent of a dress, with her hair standing up all over her head. Before she could do or say anymore, the ushers grabbed her by the arms and pulled her out, kicking and screaming.

"Let me go? Let me go right now!" She yelled while being drugged away.

"Ben, Ben!" I called for him.

Phillip and Erica helped me to my feet. I stood there in total shock. It was only when Ben turned to face me and mouthed, I'm sorry, that I turned to run out of the sanctuary. Ben chose Stacey and went after her. I wouldn't have wished this day on my worst enemy. I couldn't believe it. I sat in my dressing room for, I know, over an hour crying. No one was left to comfort me, but my mother and Erica.

"O, there will be repercussions for this." My mother said, walking back and forth.

"Mama, you're in church," I said, trying to get her to calm down.

"I -don't- give- a- damn- where I am! Don't nobody mess over my child." She snapped.

She was fighting mad. All I could do was to let her rant and rave. I love my mother dearly, but she meant what she said. Even though Ben had hurt me, I hoped for his sake he didn't run into her anytime soon. She was on a warpath. Although he was to blame for everything, we tried to explain what happened, but she wasn't hearing it.

Ms. Cookie Reed was the type of woman who took excellent care of what was hers. She had three rules. Don't mess with her child, money, or man. All in that order, and somebody had broken the first rule.

"Tamara, can I get you anything?" Erica asked, handing me more tissue.

"A gun."

"Murder is not the answer." She said.

"Well, what is it then?" Nothing made sense anymore.

"At this point, I'm not sure. Let me help you get out of this dress."

"Erica, how could anyone be so spiteful to disrupt someone's wedding?"

"Girl, I wish I knew. Not only did she bring the wedding to a halt, but she has broken up a family."

"How am I going to face all those people?" I was so embarrassed.

"Tamara, I am so sorry this has happened to you, but we will leave here with our heads held high," Erica said.

"You got that right, honey. Hey, you don't have anything to be embarrassed about. So come on, baby, change out that dress, and let's go."

"Okay, mama," I said, still sniffling.

I didn't want to change my clothes. All I wanted to do was run out of there and never look back. I tried to get as far away from this place as humanly possible. Niecy, here I come.

Chapter 2

TAMARA

This morning, I was no closer to having any of my doubts reassured, or my questions answered. This situation had rocked me to my core. Thank God, it was only a dream, but what a nightmare!

I wondered if had we waited, would the outcome be different? Feeling how I felt now, hell, yes. I would have never married Benjamin. And I guess what this all boils down to is me being angry with myself. I knew better than to allow myself to get caught up like this. I don't know if it was fear of losing him or the embarrassment of calling off our wedding the night before. I'm sure our family and friends would have understood if they knew why. At least, I hoped they would.

As I looked back over our relationship, there was no reason for us to get married so soon. We weren't the ones becoming parents. If I was honest with myself, it wasn't that he was just expecting a child. It was with whom he was expecting a child. The thought of Stacey having something I considered mine and mine alone was fueling my anger. Yes, I have the ring and the man, but she'll always have ties to him if this baby is his. Was this enough to sustain a marriage? How on earth was I going to accept his child if it were true?

Oh my God, what am I going to do? This baby mess had filled my head with so many questions it now hurt. I don't know about anything anymore. I know I should have been having the best time of my life. But all I can do is pretend, and I am tired of pretending that everything is okay when it's not. I am angry. I am angry with Ben, Stacey, and myself. But I have to give it to Ben. He has done everything within his power to make me happy, but all I can do is wonder if we made a mistake by getting married. I know I should stop complaining and thank God, because things could always be worse. Although Stacey sent that letter to me, she had not dared to show her face at my wedding, and for that, I was truly grateful. God only knows what I would've done had it ended that way.

I had to make a decision: either I was going to fight for my marriage and forgive, or I was going to be a woman about mine and tell Ben it was over. I wanted my marriage, and I loved my husband, but Ben having a baby with someone else was a little too much for me to handle. If I choose to stay, I had to let go of all these doubts and enjoy my life. I could no longer allow someone else to steal my joy and kill my peace. Slowly, I was coming to terms with not having all the answers right now, but come what may, I'll make the best decision about my future when the time comes.

I closed my eyes and said a silent prayer for better days ahead. While praying, a sense of peace came over me, and I felt like I could move forward with the hope of a better tomorrow. The main thing I prayed for was for Ben not to be the father of that baby. Stacey had slept with Ben, Terrance, Ce, and God only knows who else. She probably didn't know who the father was herself, just trifflin.

I am going to need a therapist, prayer partner, a pastor, and an exorcist to help me get through this. The more I think about her, the angrier I become. If I ever see her again, I can't be held responsible for my actions. There will not be a question of whether or not it was intentional. My peace was gone, and I was thirty-eight hot all over again.

Chapter 3

STACEY

Ring... ring... ring...

Who is this calling me this early in the morning?

"Hello!"

"Good morning, Sunshine. How are you and the little one doing this fine Sunday morning?"

"I'm sleepy and tired. Jasmine, what the hell do you want so early in the morning?" She was just too chipper for me.

"Girl, nothing. I called to see if you were going to church this morning."

"If I was going where? What time is it?"

"It's just a little after seven."

"Jazzy, why are you calling so early for? Service doesn't start until eleven."

She bet not say nothing about Sunday school.

Stacey, get up! We're not going to our church. I want to go to TJ's church."

"Who? I am not going to help you spy on TJ and his girlfriend. Leave those people alone. Besides, you have started enough trouble by writing that stupid letter."

"I didn't stir up enough trouble because they still got married. That Tamara is one stupid woman, if you ask me. I don't know not-one-female that would still marry a man after finding out he cheated on her and got the other woman pregnant. Unless she's in it for his money," she thought aloud. "If it's not, she's stupid, stupid."

"Girl, so. I don't care, that's good for her. Let her be the dumb one. It doesn't make me none, no way. Besides, I told you, I didn't know who this baby's father was anyway, but you just had to put your two cents in. People just don't know. You have everybody fooled. They think I am the one, but it's really you. The queen of schemes. You stay scheming."

"Whatever, Stacey. I just didn't want you to end up like me. I'm all alone, and my baby daddy somewhere else loving up some other woman."

"What are you talking about, Jazzy? You ran TJ off, and you know it. Plus, you got it better than most chicks I know. At least you don't have to work, and depending on who this kid's father is, I might be joining you...but that mess you pulled was foul." I had to laugh, but it really wasn't funny. She could have gotten me and my baby hurt.

"Forget that. TJ wanted to be with that stuck-up, boring-ass teacher over me. But I ain't sweating that. I was trying to help you out, but that's cool. It didn't work for you, but it got me what I wanted." She said, laughing.

"That's just sad. Leave me and my unborn child out of your sadistic games. I will go to church with you, but it won't be that one. I don't need no more trouble. I have too much going on already. I don't won't any more stares and whispers than necessary."

"I am not thinking about any of those stuck-up people. I will see you at ten o'clock."

Before I could say anything more, she hung up on me.

I don't want to cause any problems. The Harrises have been good to me. Even after they heard about Ce and me ending our engagement, Pop Harris still called to ask if there was anything he could do to help. I couldn't bring myself to tell him that I was sleeping with both of his sons. But all that is past me now. I have other things to focus on. My baby is due in three weeks. I am hoping so hard that this baby is Ben's because Terrance doesn't have a pot to piss in and a window to throw it out of. Hell, he already had a wife and two kids.

When I called Ben and told him I was pregnant, he was very understanding, and even hugged me. He told me not to worry if the baby was his. He would take care of his child. The boy didn't waste any time, though. The next thing I knew, he and Tamara were getting married. I got upset and called him out on his lies.

Come to think about it, I would be stupid as hell not to say this baby wasn't his. What I'll do is convince him this baby is his and have him sign the birth certificate before getting a DNA test. That way, if the test comes back saying the baby is not his, he'll already be the signor on the birth certificate, which would grant me at least child support from both the biological father and Ben. I have to put my plan into motion by getting him involved in this pregnancy. I should have been doing this all along. I'll call him later and ask him to carry me to my doctor's appointment. May the best daddy win. I thought to myself, smiling.

Chapter 4

BENJAMIN

I don't know what is going on, but I must somehow turn this around. What I thought was someone yelling awakened me out of my sleep. I opened my eyes, turned over, and my baby was gone. I got out of bed, grabbed my robe, and went into the bathroom to freshen up. When I returned, Tamara was still not there.

Looking around, I noticed the balcony door was open. Which only made sense for her to be out there. I remember her telling me how she loved the view of the water and the white, sandy beach.

Just as I thought, she was sitting on the balcony.

"Good morning, beautiful," I said as I stepped onto the balcony, leaning over and kissing her on the neck. I must have startled her because she jumped and looked at me as if she could kill somebody.

"Baby, what's wrong...Are you okay...Did I scare you?" I asked, reaching out to her.

"Nothing's the matter, and I'm fine. You didn't scare me." She said dryly, with a slight attitude.

"Are you sure?" She must have noticed the look of concern on my face, because her face softened slightly. She was still somewhat frowning.

"Did you sleep well?" She asked.

"Yeah, baby, I slept well, but it was not the same without my brown sugar being next to me...you dig?" She turned her head away to keep from laughing.

I knew talking as if I was from one of those Black 70s films from back in the day would make her laugh. But it was short-lived. I took her chin and gently turned her face around toward mine.

Looking into her eyes, I saw she was upset, and I wanted to know why. So I asked. "Baby, what's wrong, really?"

"Nothing, Benjamin." She said, with tears forming.

"Sweetheart, talk to me. You can tell me anything. Don't do this. Don't hide your feelings from me.

"It's just...it's just..." was all she could say before breaking down. Before I knew it, I was on my knees, kneeling down before her, holding her as tight as I possibly could.

"I'm sorry, Ben." She said, wiping her eyes, trying to pull herself together.

"Baby, you have nothing to apologize for. I just want to know what's going on. What is making my beautiful wife cry?"

"You are." Softly, she said while looking into my eyes.

"Me! How? What did I do?" I was so confused. I had to stand up.

"Ben, ever since I received that letter and those pictures, I am being terrorized in my dreams, as well as in my thoughts. I don't know what all this means. I mean, I am not sure if we did the right thing by getting married or if we moved too soon. Plus, what if you are the father...how am I to handle all of this...I just don't know anymore because...

"Whoa...whoa...wait a minute. Tamara, let's go inside and really talk about this. Because I need to reassure you of some things."

I took my wife by the hand and led her into the bedroom. We sat on the bed facing each other. "First of all, Mrs. Harris, you are my life, and second of all, I love you with all of my heart, woman. Don't you ever think us moving forward with our lives was ever a mistake? Tamara, I would never intentionally hurt you. Granted, if this child should happen to be mine, which I doubt...we will deal with it then, not before. I can't believe you don't have enough faith in us to know these things." I said, looking at her with disappointment. I was hurting because she thought our union was a mistake. When I thought I had lost her, I was on the verge of having a breakdown. I love this woman with every fiber of my body. There's nothing I wouldn't sacrifice for her. I thought she knew that.

"Ben, you can't blame me for having doubts!" She yelled.

"And I don't blame you. I want you to know we are stronger than this. You act like we met two days ago and just decided on a whim to get hitched."

"I didn't say that!" She shouted.

"Well, what are you saying?" I yelled back.

{Silence}

"Tamara, what are we doing?" I whispered. "Here we are in Montego Bay, Jamaica on our honeymoon. This is our last day here. We are supposed to be making beautiful memories, and here we are arguing over something that may not be."

I took Tamara's hands and kissed them.

"I don't want to argue with you anymore. I love you, and I am thankful for your being my wife. You are my wife for a reason, not a season, but a lifetime. I wouldn't have it any other way. Now the question is, do you believe in us?"

"Yes."

"Do you believe we can weather this storm together?"

"Yes."

"Do you believe you can forgive me for getting angry?"

"Yes."

"Do you love me?"

"Yes."

"Do you think I love you?"

"I don't know." She said with a slight giggle.

"Really. Well, do you think I can show you how much I love you?"

Before she could answer, I started kissing her passionately. We made love that morning. I could not express in words alone the way I felt for her. I knew I could eventually remove all of her doubts by showing her one hard, long stroke at a time.

Chapter 5

STACEY

I was so uncomfortable standing here. Service was finally over, and I was so ready to go. I was just waiting my turn to walk out in the aisle to leave. I let Jasmine talk me into coming to St. Peter's. I was praying their parents didn't see me. Now I know why Big Mama always said to be precise about what you asked God for in prayer, because I forgot to mention Christopher's name, and there he was.

"Thank you for lettin-

"Stacey!" He said, interrupting me.

"Yes, it's me." I was over this conversation already.

"Girl, what in the world…is there something I should know?" He asked with a grim look on his face.

"No, it isn't. So you can stop looking at me like that."

"Thank God for that. What are you doing here, anyway?"

"If you must know, I was attending service with my cousin. She comes here from time to time, and if memory serves me correctly, we were supposed to get married in this very church, remember?"

"How could I forget?" He asked sarcastically.

Now I was pissed off.

"You know what, Ce? It was nice to see you again, and I hope you have a great freakin' life," I said as I tried to storm away from him, belly and all.

"Stacey, wait. I didn't mean nothing by it. I was just shocked to see you. have moved on with my life, and I can see you have done the same...so there's no need for any unpleasantries." I knew he didn't mean a word of it. His body language gave it away.

"Whatever, Ce," I said, trying to walk away.

"Wait...wait. To prove no hard feelings, tell me where you're registered, and I'll have my new fiancée send you a baby gift." He said, still being sarcastic with a smirk on his face.

At that point, I wanted to cuss him slap out, but his father's nosey parishioners, Ms. Birdie and Ms. Alfreda, were in earshot distance, talking to Jasmine. I just did the next best thing. I flipped him off and walked out.

"Looks like that has already been done." He said, laughing.

By this time, I stopped in my tracks and was about to make an about-face when Jasmine grabbed me by the arm, and pulled my fat butt out of the church.

"Girl, are you crazy? Flipping people off in church."

"Jazzy, you didn't know what he was saying to me and the way he looked at me. Like I was some washed-up hoe or something. Uh-uh, I'm not having it."

"Stacey, stop. You are getting upset, plus that's not good for the baby. I'm just glad I stopped you before you could really do some damage."

"All I was going to do was invite him to his nephew's baby shower," I said as I buckled my seatbelt.

"Girl, you mean to tell me he does not know what went down between you and his brother."

"I'm not sure. I don't see why Christopher wouldn't, but we can find out."

"How?"

"Quick, give me one of my baby shower invitations. I got something for his butt."

"Stacey, what are you about to do?"

"You'll see. Pull up next to that black Mercedes before he gets in." She pulled up right next to him. I rolled down my window.

"Hey, Ce."

"Stacey, what do you want now?"

He was trying to flex because he had his new chick with him. She looked like an overly made Bratz doll.

"Nothing much. I forgot to give you an invitation." I said as I handed him the invitation.

"Girl, I know you have lost your mind. I'm not coming to any baby shower."

"No, I haven't. It's not for you. Tell your folks so they won't miss their first grandson's baby shower."

"You said the baby wasn't mine." He said with an angry look.

"I know. It's not. It's Benjamin's. **He was a better lover than you!**" I shouted. I rolled up the window just in time. He threw the invitation back at me, but it hit the glass instead. I missed the rest of what he had to say because Jazzy was speeding out of the parking lot, and I was laughing

way too hard to even care.

25

Chapter 6

BENJAMIN

I don't know what the hell is going on back in the Ham, but I am not talking to anyone until my feet hit the ground of Birmingham-Shuttlesworth International Airport. They were blowing my phone up. If Ce hadn't called me at least five times, I knew TJ had called me ten. The only person who hadn't called was Phillip, and if he had called, I would know something was definitely wrong. They probably don't want anything too tough, no way.

I am glad Tamara is not upset anymore. I can understand her being upset, but man, I'm doing the best I knew how. She never thought about how I was handling this. Hell, I don't even know how I'm handling this. I never thought I would ever be in this situation. I thought Stacey was out of my life for good, but it seems she is going to be around for a while. One thing I am going to do is handle my busy differently than TJ. He was having his ice cream and cake, too, sometimes on the same day. I'm not with that.

The first thing I want from Stacey is a DNA test. There's no way I'm doing anything without one. How am I going to tell my parents? Oh my God, Ce! What am I supposed to say to this man? "Oh, sorry, bro, I slept with your ex-fiancée, and now she's having my baby." Man, please, I wouldn't want to hear that junk either. I am glad that I had come clean with Ce in the beginning, but I didn't want this situation to cause me to lose my brother or my wife. What am I going to do now? The baby is due in a few weeks. I don't know what she's having or anything. Man, this is so messed up. I've always wanted children. I can see myself having a son to groom and a daughter to spoil.

"What are you over there smiling about?" Tamara asked.

"Oh...huh?" I pretended not to hear her.

"What are you over there so starry-eyed and smiling about?"

"Just our future, baby."

"It must be wonderful if you're smiling like that."

"With you in my life, it will be," I said, leaning over and giving her a kiss.

"What are you getting ready to do? It will take us a minute to reach the States, so what do you have planned?"

"Nothing, really. I was going to read this magazine I bought and listen to some music."

"Sounds good, sweetie. If you don't mind, I would like to review some information Phillip sent me. He is interested in us investing in this luxury car dealership."

"Oh yeah, where?"

"In Dallas."

"Is it profitable?"

"Very."

"What's the delay?"

"None. I just want to be sure."

"Well, when will I see those figures?"

"Soon, I promise."

That's another thing I loved about Tamara. She could flip from being my wife to our corporation's account manager in a nino-second. She got a promotion on her own merit without any influence from Phillip or me. I was and am very proud of my beautiful wife.

Chapter 7

TAMARA

I was feeling guilty when Ben started working. I brought my laptop along, but I had no intentions of using it. Ben, being the down low work alcoholic that he is, jumped right into his work. I admired him for so many things, but when it came down to business, he was about his. I put my AirPods in and allowed Boney James to blow me away while watching the busy bee go. The only time he stopped was to answer his phone. He had a weird look when he saw the caller ID. Then, he had done something I never once witnessed him do. He answered his phone, stood, and walked to the bathroom.

I know like hell he didn't leave, so that I couldn't hear him. I pulled my earbuds out and walked toward the bathroom. The last word I heard him say was, "I will be there."

"You'll be where, Sweetie?" I asked him as he opened the bathroom door.

"Tamara, how long were you standing outside the door?" He looked surprised.

"Ever-dent-ly, not long enough to get a straight answer."

"Huh...what are you talking about?"

"Who was that on the phone?"

"TJ."

"Since when do you start checking the caller ID and getting up to hold a conversation."

"Right around the same time you started eavesdropping."

He had me there. I couldn't say anything. So, I let him win that one.

"If you must know, TJ has called me about ten times, and Ce has called at least five. I wanted to know what was going on that they had to call me so much."

"Interesting. You usually just answer the phone based on TJ's special ring. Now you are checking the caller ID? Alrighty then."

"Tamara, either you're going to believe me or you won't, but I'm not going to argue with you about it."

"Okay, prove it."

"Prove what?"

"Let me see your cell phone."

"I'm not showing you anything. If you don't believe me, call him on your phone and ask him."

"Fine, I'll just do that!"

He thought I was playing. Something told me that the call wasn't from TJ.

Ring...ring...ring

"Hello."

"Hey TJ...when was the last time you spoke to my husband?"

"Minutes ago. I wanted to know when you guys were coming home...what's that?"

"Nothing...how is Erica?"

"She's fine."

"Oh, okay then. I'll call her when I get home. We will see you guys soon...bye."

"Bye," TJ said.

"So, did that satisfy your curiosity?" Ben asked sarcastically.

"No, it didn't."

"Okay, Tamara, whatever you say or whatever you want to think. I told you from the beginning, you have to trust me."

I had nothing else to say to him because I felt like he was hiding something from me. I was going to occupy the rest of my time by talking to my mother. He went back to what he was doing, as if my feelings meant nothing. Selfish son-of-a bi...

"Hello, Mama." It was so good to hear her voice.

"Hey, baby. How are you and that new son-in-law of mine doing?"

"We're fine, Mama. I was calling to let you know we were heading back?"

"Un-huh. What's wrong, Tammie?"

"Nothing Ma..."

"Un-huh, I know when something is wrong with my child. I can hear it in your voice."

"I'm fine, I promise. I'm just a little tired...that's all."

"Un-huh. Well, did you have a good time?"

"I did, and I bought you something, too."

"Chile, you didn't have to go and do that...but since you did. What did you bring me?" She said, laughing with that thick Louisiana accent of hers.

"I know you want to know, but you will have to wait and see."

"For how long? When will you be coming home, baby?"

"I'm not sure." I was coming home this weekend, but I wanted it to be a surprise.

"Aww, okay then." She said sadly.

"What were you doing?"

"Brushing honey butter over these yeast rolls."

"Ooh Mama, I hadn't had any of those in so long."

"Try coming home sometimes. I make them every day...you know."

"Fine, I will see you Friday."

"Are you serious?"

"Yes, ma'am, I will be there first thing Friday morning." I hadn't been home in over a year.

"Hey Carolyn, my baby is coming home, chile." She told her assistant. "Are you driving, flying, or what?"

"I haven't decided yet, but I will let you know?"

"Is Ben coming too?"

Looking over at him, I replied the best way I could. "Probably not. He has so many things to do. Private, secretive matters, and all." I said, looking directly at him, but he didn't say a word.

"Huh?"

"Nothing, Mama, but I will call you with all the details. Love you, Ma."

"Love you too, baby...bye."

I went back to listening to my music and reading my magazine until our plane landed.

Chapter 8

BENJAMIN

It was killing me to lie to Tamara. I was so glad TJ and I had created that system years ago. It was flawless. Tamara was right to be suspicious. Stacey had called to ask me to go with her to her doctor's appointment. I agreed, thinking nothing more of it, but I knew I couldn't tell Tamara the truth when I came out of the bathroom. She would go ballistic over something so innocent. I thought she was being very childish, but I was going to let her have that because I knew I had just lied to her.

I was happy to hear that the plane had landed safely and we could unbuckle our seatbelts to exit the plane. I don't think I could take another minute more of this. As soon as I get home, I am heading to Horizons to have a glass of Hennessey.

We departed our private aircraft and rode home in silence. It took us exactly twenty minutes to get home.

"Home sweet home," I said aloud.

"I don't know how sweet it is?" She replied.

"As sweet as you make it, my dear."

"And you?"

"I'll always be sweet to you," I said, trying to kiss her on the neck.

"Move, because I'm still upset with you." She said, acting like she wanted to push me back.

"You don't want me to move for real."

"Stop before the driver sees us."

"Girl, that man is not thinking about us. Hurry up and get out of this car so we can go make-up.

We rushed out of that SUV like we were in a foot race.

"Well, Mrs. Harris, may I have the honor of carrying you over the threshold?"

"Yes, you may."

I carried her inside. Everything was just as I left it that night she left, plus the other gifts we received. I put her down and gave her a tight hug and kiss while the driver placed our bags inside of the house.

"Honey, why don't you take the bags upstairs while I look through the gifts?" She suggested.

"It would be more fun if you left all this stuff down here and joined me upstairs."

"I'm sure it would be, but I want to see what we got." She said, whining.

"Fine, be that way, but when you do walk those sexy hips up these stairs, you'll owe me double," I said, kissing those sexy soft lips of hers. I bent over to pick up the suitcases, and everything in my pocket fell out.

"Don't worry, I'll get that. You just go ahead and take those suitcases upstairs since I'm paying you."

I couldn't wait. I grabbed our luggage, flew upstairs, and hurried back in that same fashion, but when I got there, she was no longer in the living room.

"Tamara...Tamara, where are you?" Walking in the kitchen, there she stood with my phone in her hand.

"Did you think that I was stupid!?" She yelled.

"What are you talking about now?"

"I'm talking about Stacey calling your lying ass and you walking off to talk to her...and before you lie, I called the number back."

"Tamara, I can explain."

"There's nothing to explain." She said, grabbing her keys and purse and heading for the garage door.

"Tamara, wait, don't leave!" She kept walking. I couldn't stop her. I was caught, and now she was gone.

Chapter 9

TAMARA

It took all I had not to slap him. I am so hurt. He lied directly to my face. If he lied about that, it's no telling what else he has lied about. I looked down and noticed my phone flashing. This could only be one person.

"What do you want?"

"Where are you going?" Ben asked.

"Out."

"What time will you be coming back so that we can discuss this?"

"Why, so you can lie to me again? I can't believe you."

"Tamara, please turn around and come back home."

"No," I replied.

"Look, Tamara, I can understand why you are upset. I apologize for lying to you, but I don't regret the reason why I did it."

"So you just think it's okay to lie to me and everything will be okay because you had a good reason. That is a bunch of nonsense, and you know it."

"Say what you will. It's the truth. I'm tired of fighting with you. I just hope you remember that I love you, and we can overcome anything if you try."

Oh no, his ass didn't just hang that phone up on me. He lies to me and then hangs up the phone like it's my fault. I have got to calm down. I thought as I tried to maneuver through traffic. I couldn't even see straight. I needed to talk to someone. I needed Erica.

Ring...ring...ri...

"Girl, what are you doing home so soon, Mrs. Newlywed?"

"About to commit murder one."

"Excuse me...what happened?"

"I don't know where to start. Where are you?"

"Just leaving school. Where are you?"

"I'm sitting in my car in the parking lot of Walk-On's," I said, sniffling.

"Tam, don't cry. I'm on my way. What happened?"

"It started from the time I said I do."

"What do you mean?"

"I had been having some doubts...and decided to give my marriage a shot...then he answered his phone...and lied about who he was talking to...and I found out it was Stacey."

"Aww, Sweetie, I'm so sorry to hear that. Look, I am ten minutes away. Pull yourself together, and I will be right there. I need to pay attention to the road. I just ran two red lights. Stop crying. I'm on my way."

"Okay, bye," I said, sniffling.

"Bye."

I looked down at my phone, and Ben was calling me back. I started not to answer the phone, but did anyway.

"Hello," I said, trying to muffle my sniffles.

"Baby, where are you? I am coming to pick you up. Enough is enough."

"I'm fine, Ben. I just need to be by myself."

"Tamara, we need each other. That is the only way we are going to make it through this."

"Ben, why didn't you tell me the truth from the beginning?"

"Because you would do this. I knew you weren't going to handle knowing she called me well, so I decided not to tell you."

"What did she want?"

"She wanted me to go with her to the doctor. That's all."

"And what did you say?"

"I told her I would go."

"Why would you do that?"

"Because I figured, what if the baby is mine? I wouldn't have attended any of her prenatal appointments or anything, plus it was something I really wanted to be there for. I want to be there for my child every step of the way."

"Your child, huh? Not too long ago, you doubted that the child was even yours. Now, all of a sudden, you are acting like it is."

"No, that's not what I'm saying."

"Well, what are you trying to say? Either it is, or it isn't."

"Tamara, I won't know until the baby is born. But just in case it is, I at least want to attend one prenatal appointment."

"Ben, you can attend whatever you want. Both you and Stacey can go to hell!"

I hung up the phone and turned it off before he could call me back. I can't believe that bastard had the nerve to tell me, his wife of nine days, about going to another woman's prenatal appointment. And his stupid ass doesn't even know if it's his child.

Chapter 10

ERICA

Who is this calling me now? Oh no, it isn't.

"Hello, Ben," I said with much attitude.

"Sis, don't sound like that."

"Sound like what? All I know is my best friend is sitting in her car crying her eyes out over your stupid butt."

"Erica, come on, man. You don't know what's going on. You are only hearing one side of the story."

"Possibly, but she's the one crying, and you're not."

"Sis, please just listen before you pass judgment, okay?"

"Listening." I was going to side with my girl no matter what. Men were all the same.

"Okay, it started when we were on the last day of our honeymoon. She was upset about Stacey being pregnant. She was saying crazy stuff like maybe us getting married was a mistake and how she was full of doubts. So I basically told her that I understood and that we would work through it blah, blah, blah."

"Un-huh."

"Well, we get on the plane headed home, and my cell phone rings. Okay, I looked at the phone because I didn't recognize the number, and when I answered, it was Stacey. All she wanted me to do was go with her to her doctor's visit. No problem, I thought, until I went into the bathroom."

"Why did you do that? You made yourself look suspicious."

"Well, okay, I did. But had she not been acting so crazy, I wouldn't have had to do that."

"Un-huh."

"Basically, I lied about who I was talking to. When we got home, she went through my phone and dialed the number back, and here we are."

That's my girl. She'll check that phone in a heartbeat.

"Ben, I mean…I don't know what to say. You should have told the truth in the beginning instead of hiding-"

"Sis, I know that." He said, cutting me off. "All I need is for my wife to come home, but she won't talk to me. So please do your brother a favor and talk some sense into her. Tell her I only love her, and she should come home. Please, Erica, I'm begging you."

"I can't make any promises, but I'll see what I can do."

"Thank you, Sis. I'll owe you one."

"Just make it payable to Erica Jones at any number of your choice, followed by a lot of zeros."

"I love you, Sis. Thanks."

"Whatever, bye."

I don't know how much he thought I was going to be able to do. It's not easy talking to a mad black woman. Her not coming home was the least of his worries. He forgot she had his Amex card and liked to go to the mall for retail therapy. Poor, dumb, dumb.

Chapter 11

TAMARA

Finally, Erica was here. She parked her car next to mine. I know I must have looked like a hot mess by the concerned expression on her face.

"Girl, are you okay? Did he hit you?" She was almost beside herself.

"No, and not physically."

"Tam, tell me what the hell is going on."

"I would love to, but first, I need a drink or two." We walked into the restaurant and placed our orders with the waiter.

"Okay, girl, let's hear it."

"Erica, I don't know what to say. I mean, he has someone pregnant, and I don't know how to handle it."

"What do you mean, he has someone pregnant? We don't know that for sure, plus, we both know that child could belong to anyone."

"That's true, but it just seems so crazy, you know. I thought about how we met and how we moved from exchanging phone numbers to exchanging vows within a matter of months. What I don't understand is why the rush?"

"I'm still lost. Help me out."

"What I'm saying is, I'm starting to realize some things."

"Like what?"

"Ben had been lying to me the whole time we were together. He said he had not cheated on me, but he had. Plus, his latest lie to me about who he was on the phone with."

"What...when?" She said with her eyes bucking.

"Ben and I started seeing each other in January, and we just got married. It's a ten-month difference. So whether he is that child's father or not, he had slept with her a month or two into our relationship."

"Oh, my God." She said, covering her mouth. "Why would he do that? You know men can be so stupid at times."

"Tell me about it. I feel like a fool. I tried to come clean about Marcus, but he wouldn't allow me to. He had been walking around here acting like nothing was happening, like he had done nothing wrong. I should have followed my first mind and confronted his cheating butt, but I allowed my heart to dictate my actions."

"So now what?" Erica asked.

"That's the question?"

"The way Ben was talking, he was trying to protect you and your feelings."

"My feelings...huh. When did you talk to him?"

I should have known he would call her. They are close.

"I talked to him on my way over here. He wants you to come home so you two can talk this out, but frankly, I don't know. From what you have said and from what he told me, I don't know if you really have a reason to go back."

"So what are you saying, Erica? I should just leave the love of my life to some other woman? Why should I let her have something that's rightfully mine? We both have made mistakes."

"Exactly!"

Ooh, I hated it when she did that to me. Erica should really be a psychiatrist rather than a teacher. She has a way of making you pour out your innermost feelings. She never tells you what you should do. She allows you to make your own decisions. She never gives her opinion because she says people are going to do what they want, anyway. They're just looking for someone to validate what they were already thinking.

"You know, you really make me sick with that." I couldn't help but laugh.

"All I wanted you to see is that your marriage was worth fighting for."

"You're right, but I still have something bothering me."

"What's that?"

"I still need to know whose baby this is."

"How in the world are you going to find that out?"

"I don't know, but I'll find out. You can believe that. How much do I owe you?"

"A nice Hermes bag will do." She said with a smile.

"If you stepped into that school building with a Hermes bag on your shoulders, those nosey folks will start saying TJ is selling drugs out of his barbershop."

"I wished they would start a rumor like that."

"You know it's true. You remember what happened when you came back to work with that new Lexus TJ bought for you?"

"I know. That was so funny. Some of them left their classrooms to go outside to look at it. People, please, it's just a car." Erica said, shaking her head.

"It's so sad that you can't have nice things and people are happy for you."

"That's the way of the world, I guess." She said.

"They could easily have the same, but it'll just cost them an arm and a leg, unlike TJ, who got his at wholesale price." I said.

"Honey, a few of them didn't even speak to me after that."

We laughed and talked more. I appreciated Erica. She's the closest thing I had to a sister. A Hermes bag is nothing compared to her being there for me, no matter what. I hoped Ben could forgive me for running out on him.

Chapter 12

BENJAMIN

I hope Erica can help me. I didn't want to involve her or TJ, but Tamara wouldn't listen to me. But why should she? I lied about Stacey countless times. I just hope she will return home. What I needed more than anything was a glass, ice, and a lot of liquid persuasion. Horizons wasn't crowded yet, but it will be, especially since happy hour is just getting started.

"Fellas," I said, walking over to our usual table.

"You mean to tell us she's going to let you come outside and play with us?" Phillip said.

"Whatever, I'm my own man. Nobody tells me what to do."

"Yeah, that's that junk he is talking now, but let her call. He'll knock us all down trying to get out of here," TJ said while they all laughed.

"Man, forget y'all. I'm in no mood to be clowned." I said in frustration.

I didn't need them clowning me. I had too much on my plate.

"Whew...what is wrong with you?" Ce asked.

"Man, you don't want to know."

"Let us guess?" All at the same time, they said, "Stacey."

"How did y'all know?"

"Man, Stacey and TJ's baby mama showed up at church

yesterday," Ce said.

"Why?"

"Well, let's say one came to spy on TJ's butt and the other, well, I really don't know." Ce said.

"What happened?" I asked, concerned.

Ce went on to explain the chain of events.

"Now Pop wants to see you." He said.

"Me...for what?"

"Call him and see Ben. Better now than later."

"Man, I don't need this mess right now. I swear, I don't."

"How's Tamara handling all this?" Phillip asked.

"She's not man, and the sad thing about all of this is, there's nothing else I can do to protect her. If I keep anything away from her, she would say I was hiding things and keeping secrets, and then if I told her everything, she would have resentment. So right now, I'm between a rock and a hard place, with no relief in sight."

"Not until that baby is born, that is," said TJ. "Once that baby is born, and the test is done, that's it. If it shows you're not the father, then you're home free. How long does she have before the baby is due?"

"I'm not sure. I think in a couple of weeks, but I'll be going with her to her prenatal appointment on Friday."

"Make sure you ask that doctor how soon you can get that DNA test done, so the trick can't pull nothing. You know I've been around that family a long time, and those broads are slicker than a can of oil."

"Sounds like you are a little upset, TJ. Is your ice cream melting?"

"Man, forget you, aight."

Now he knew how I felt. It was my turn to laugh at him.

"Ah, nah, man. It was funny as hell when it was me, right?"

"Hmm," Phillip said, shaking his head. "For this reason, I'm so glad that I'm not seriously attached."

"Negro say what?! You are not attached because yo butt is scared of a real commitment." TJ told him.

"I wouldn't say all that. I'm just selective."

"Man, you wit that mess this evening, I see," TJ said to Phillip.

"That fine ass woman you got. Why wouldn't you want to settle down with her?" Ce asked Phillip.

"Because he's scared. He won't even give her a promise pinky ring, scary butt." I said.

"I wanna see what's all out here first. You know, make sure I haven't overlooked anyone."

We all just looked at Phillip for a minute and then burst out laughing because he was full of it.

"For real, Ben, you need to call Pop. He was really upset, bro, and I don't think delaying the matter is going to make it better. He talked to me for thirty minutes about how I should have conducted myself on church grounds in front of the other members. Then TJ got a call."

"Yeah, man. He talked to me for forty-five minutes about being a family man versus a lady's man. And I hadn't done anything. So now it is your turn. Good luck." TJ said, patting me on my back.

I needed to talk to Pop, anyway. I needed some help and direction. I decided to call when I was on my way home.

Ring...ring...ring...

"Praise the Lord."

"Hey, Ma," I said, thanking God, she answered.

"Benji, is that you?"

"Yes, ma'am. It's me."

"How was your honeymoon?"

"It was just fine. Tamara and I brought some gifts back with us. I will come by later this week and drop them off."

"Oh, baby, you didn't have to do that."

"I know, Ma, where's Pop?" I asked. I may as well get the lecturing part over with, so that I can get the help that I need.

"Oh, child, he's in his study. You want to talk to him?"

"Yes, ma'am." She just didn't know how badly.

"Well, hold on, I'll get him for you." Greg, she called in the distance.

"Hello."

"Hey, Pop. Ce said-"

"Yes, I want to speak to you, son." He didn't let me get another word out. "Son, I don't know what is going on, and furthermore, I don't understand why it was brought to the church."

"Well-"

"Well, I understand you may have something to do with all this. I hope you have something to say for yourself."

"But-"

"But nothing! You two have brought shame and scandal to the church's doorstep."

"Pop, if you give me a chance, I will explain."

"I'm listening. What do you have to say for yourself?"

"We never meant to bring any shame or scandal to the church. We didn't have anything to do with that."

"So are you saying that young lady was lying, that you are not her baby's father?"

"Yes and no, Pop."

"What kind of answer is that!?"

"Just let me finish. It started when I met Tamara. She was the only one that I wanted to be with. So, I broke off my relationship with Stacey to be with Tamara.

Needless to say, she didn't take it too well. When we had our company's party, she showed up on the arm of Ce. I never knew, nor was I ever told, that she was engaged to Ce. She later told him, that she had an affair and broke off their engagement. Seeing how hurt he was, I told him everything. Not knowing if it would destroy our family."

"So, I guess my question now is, whose baby is it?" Pop asked.

"That answer, Pop, we won't know until she has the baby."

"Oh my goodness, and my poor daughter. How is she doing?"

"Not too good. We had a huge argument earlier today."

"Over what?"

"I lied about talking to Stacey. All I wanted to do Pop was protect her and not hurt her anymore than I had already. Now, I don't know if she's coming home, because she won't even talk to me."

"Sometimes, son, you have to allow time to heal the wound. No matter how apologetic you are, you must understand her position in this. She loves you, son, and for that reason, she will return. You must allow her space to make her own decisions despite your wanting to protect her."

"Thanks Pop. You are always there for us when we need you."

"Well, why was I the last to know about this scandal? If that girl hadn't come to the church, I'd still be in the dark."

"Sorry."

"Sorry, my a-. Boy, get off my phone. I'm all upset again. You had better do right by my Tamara."

"Your Tamara?"

"Yes, that's what I said. She is the daughter I've always wanted, and your mother feels the same way. Hurt her again, and I will have Ms. Cookie come to your house and lay hands on you."

"Please don't do that, Pop. I have enough problems. I don't need Tamara's mom beating me up, too."

"God bless and stay prayerful, son. Everything will work out."

"Love you, Pop."

"Love you too, son. Goodnight."

My dad made me feel like I had won a million dollars, but reality sat back in. Will she be there when I get home? Ten minutes away from home, there was only one thing I could do.

Ring...ring...

"Hello."

"Hi."

"Sweetheart, are you home?" I asked her.

"Where else was I going?"

"Baby, I'm so sorry, I didn't-"

"It's okay, Ben, just come home. I need you."

"I'm on the way. What were you doing?"

"Thinking of you." She said seductively.

"Please don't sound like that. You are going to make me hit something or somebody."

"Where are you?"

"Around the corner. Why?"

"Because you need to beg my forgiveness over and over again."

"I will be doing that and then some."

"Hur-ry up before I start without you."

"You can hang up now. I'm here."

Add a little sugar, honeysuckle lamb...was all I heard when I walked in. Oh no, she wasn't up in here...candles glowing everywhere...

Gladys Knight was singing through the surround sound system. Setting the

mood as Tamara begged my pardon over and over again.

55

Chapter 13

BENJAMIN

Life as I knew it couldn't get any better. Tamara and I made up and discussed our Stacey situation. I told her that I would call Stacey and cancel, but as fate would have it, I didn't have to tell her about cancelling with Stacey after all. I know, I promised not to keep things from her, but I thought this would be for the best. I had some questions that I needed answers to. Besides, I didn't want to ruin her trip to see her mom. After dropping Tamara off at the airport, I had just enough time to pick up Stacey and have her on time for her appointment. Who would have thought me of all people would be coming back here?

Ring...rin-

"Hey, Ben!"

"I'm outside."

"Don't you want to come in for a minute?" She asked.

"Nope, traffic will pick up soon, so come on out."

I hung up the phone before she could say anything else. Seeing her come out, I was glad I drove Tamara's car. Stacey was literally wobbling. She looked like she could go into labor at any moment.

"Thank you, Ben, for taking me. It's hard for me to get behind my steering wheel."

"No problem, but first things first, I don't appreciate that drama you and your cousin pulled at my dad's church, and I don't appreciate you trying to stop my wedding, either."

"If I told you I had nothing to do with either incident, would you have believed me, no? You wouldn't because you have no idea how my personal life has been affected by all of this. Let's get a few things straight: I never tried to stop your wedding. I didn't care who you married, and I didn't start that mess at the church. Christopher did. I would never do that to your parents. They were good to me, unlike you and your brother."

"Whatever you did, or did not do, make sure it doesn't happen again. You may not like the results the next time." I said, pulling off from her home.

"Are you threatening me?"

"No, baby, it's a promise," I said with a clenched jaw.

"All I wanted to do was to allow you an opportunity to be a part of this child's life before and after. If you didn't want that, all you simply had to say was no thank you." She said, crying.

I couldn't help but feel sorry for her. I was a little harsh, but I meant every single word I had said.

"Stacey, look, I'm sorry everything had to come to this, but you know...we didn't end on good terms, and out of the blue, I get a phone call, and then with what occurred recently, you know I have to take a stance."

"But that's the thing. I didn't want anything to do with you per se. I just thought you should know that I was pregnant." She said, still sniffling.

"We won't discuss this anymore. I don't want you upset. I know it's not good for you or the baby, so just calm down."

"That's fine by me. I don't want Dr. Morgan to put me back in the hospital."

"Put you back in the hospital?"

"Yeah, I had lost my job, and my blood pressure went through the roof, so she slapped my rump in the hospital for a few days."

"I'm sorry to hear that. Why did you lose your job?"

"I'd rather not discuss that. What I need right now is to just calm down." She said.

"So my brother tells me you are having a baby shower tomorrow?"

"Yeah, I am. Could you do me a favor after we leave the doctor's office?"

"Sure, what do you need?"

"Umm, I wanted to look at my baby's wish list. Now, my old co-workers will probably get me the stuff I asked for, but my family. They wouldn't do right if right were in them."

I couldn't help but laugh because I knew she was telling the truth.

After I dropped Stacey off in front of the hospital, I parked Tamara's car in the hospital's parking deck. I had to make sure I had the parking stub in hand for two reasons.

One, Stacey said the front office would validate my parking stub, and two, I didn't want to leave the stub behind for Tamara to find. I met Stacey in the hospital lobby, and I must say it didn't take them long to call her back. I sat in the waiting room for ten minutes when I was told I could go to the room and be with her.

This experience was something I had hoped for, but not with the one I was sharing it with. I dreamt of the day Tamara and I would conceive. I could hardly wait. That's why I made it a sure shot every time she and I are together. I don't know if she knew it or not, but I purposely worked it out for a reason, as if we had to replenish the earth ourselves. We were listening to the strong and rhythmic heartbeat of the baby. I couldn't help but wonder how big he was going to be. Stacey was a small framed woman, and her frame had stretched from five to ten. This couldn't be comfortable for her, I'm sure. I would have thought she was having twins or something, if I didn't know any better. So I asked the tech.

"Are you guys sure it's just one baby in there?"

Laughing, she replied, "We are pretty sure, but you can never tell. There have been those rare occasions when the-"

"Look, I know that both of you find this entertaining, but ain't a damn thing funny," she said, interrupting the tech.

"Whoa, potty-mouth." That only made matters worse. The tech and I laughed harder than before.

"I'm sorry. We were just joking with you. I like him, Stacey. You should have brought him around sooner." No reply came from her, so the tech continued, "Well, Dr. Morgan will be in shortly. Is there anything I can get for you?"

"No, thank you, Meghan, I'm fine," Stacey said.

"Well, if I don't see you before you leave, have a great day. Goodbye, sir it was nice to meet you."

"Likewise," I replied, but the truth of the matter was that we weren't introduced formally from the beginning. Now that think about it, that may not have been such a bad idea after all.

Now, it was just Stacey and I. She didn't say anything, so I guess she was mad.

"Hey, why are you so quiet?" I asked.

"No reason. I'm just waiting on Dr. Morgan so I can go home."

"So you no longer want me to take you to Baby's World anymore?" I asked.

"No, you don't have to. I'll get my cousin or somebody else to take me."

"Anyone but me, huh?"

"If you say so." She said nonchalantly.

At that time, there was a knock at the door.

"Come in," Stacey replied.

"Good morning, Stacey." Her doctor said with the brightest smile.

"Good morning, Dr. Morgan." She said dryly.

"What's wrong with my mother-to-be?"

"Nothing?"

"Yes, it is. Tell me?" She asked, looking at me with a smile.

"Well, he and Meghan were in here talking about twins and stuff. I can't take care of two babies. What am I going to do with two babies?" She said, crying.

"Ah, Stacey, calm down. You know there is only one little boy in there. He's just going to be a big baby, that's all. Trust me, if there were two, you would have delivered long before now...and who do we have here, causing you to have all this anxiety today?"

"Hello, Dr. Morgan. My name is Ben, and I am here with Stacey because she needed someone to bring her, so here I am."

"Un-huh. So you're the young man that I've heard so much about."

That caught me by a total surprise.

"I'm not sure what all you have heard," I said, looking at Stacey.

"But I do have some questions."

"Sure, what can I answer for you?"

"Well, Dr. Morgan, how soon can we have a DNA test done on the baby?"

Stacey's eyes shot from me to Dr. Morgan. The look on her face told it all. It didn't go unnoticed. Dr. Morgan was patting Stacey's leg as she replied.

"Ben, that is an excellent question. A DNA test can be done now, if-"

"No, the hell it won't. Nobody is testing my baby for anything until he is born, and that's that." Stacey said before Dr. Morgan could finish.

"Stacey, you will need to calm down and relax, or you will stay here at the hospital until you deliver." She said sternly to her. "To finish answering your question Ben, we don't suggest having a DNA test done before the baby is born, unless we have a serious reason to do so, and unfortunately, proof of paternity is not a suitable cause in my opinion."

"I understand, Dr. Morgan. I just needed to know how and when to proceed."

"Have I answered all of your questions?"

"Yes, ma'am."

"Good. Stacey, don't be embarrassed. At least he had the decency to ask in person. Some people try to request such things in the first trimester. It's not until we explain that it is a very dangerous procedure that they back off. It could put the mother and child in harm's way."

This lady was good. She examined Stacey, talked to me, and relaxed her all at the same time.

"Well, sweetie, this baby is coming real soon. You have dilated two centimeters. It won't be long now." A look of fear appeared on Stacey's face. I gave Stacey's hand a gentle squeeze when I noticed how scared she actually was.

"Dr. Morgan, are you saying I could have this baby within the next two weeks?"

"Yes, that's exactly what I'm saying. You can deliver at any time.

Get plenty of rest. Stay off those feet, and if you need anything, call us. It was nice to meet you, Ben. I hope everything turns out well for you.”

“Either way, Dr. Morgan, everything will be fine,” I said, hoping for the best.

I stepped outside the room while Stacey put her clothes back on. When she came out, we got the parking ticket stamped and walked in silence. She waited for me to bring the car around, and while I was doing so, I started to feel a little excited, but of course, I didn’t want to get too caught up because there was still a very strong possibility that this baby was not mine. Pulling the car around, I helped Stacey into the car. She hadn’t really said much since we left the doctor’s office.

“Are you okay?” I asked her.

“I’m fine. It’s just hitting me that my baby will be here soon, and I will be all alone. That’s the hardest part...I’m all alone.” She said.

“Stacey, you know if the baby is mine, I’ll be there for you.”

“And I appreciate that, Ben. I really do, but I don’t want to cause you any problems, either.”

“Either way, Stacey, either way.” Changing the subject, “I know you were told to take it easy, but I would love to take you to Baby’s World.”

“Really!” She said excitedly. “Well, I’m kinda hungry too, but if you want to go now, I’m game.”

“Girl, just in case that baby is mine, you are going to eat now.”

“You’re already being an overprotective father, but seriously, I’d rather see what's left on that list, then eat."

"Alright, it's your call, ma'am."

"Shopping." She said.

I pulled into the store's parking lot just in time to have my heart to fall into my left shoe. I was watching some of Pop's nosiest church members cross in front of us. They were walking to their car. Thank God, I decided to drive Tamara's car. It had tinted windows, and it was not flashy. I could have been anyone, and for that reason, I was thankful. All I needed was Sister Carla to see me. She and her daughter Alisha were just leaving the store.

Sister Carla had no reason to talk about anybody, but she did. Her daughter had four kids and five baby daddies. The fifth child had not been born yet. Years ago, Sister Carla wanted to say I was the father of the first child. What Alisha failed to tell her mother was not only did we sleep together, but I was also wearing not one condom but two. She was the biggest freak in high school. She became pregnant our senior year in high school. Sister Carla thought she had hit the jackpot, but DNA told a different story, and she hadn't liked my family or me ever since. Why she still attends our church is beyond me. I guess it's just to make our lives a living hell. That's why Pop was so upset about that Stacey fiasco. That spectacle gave Sister Carla something to talk about. Other than that, she really had nothing to say about us too tough unless it was that run-of-the-mill old-fashioned hating. I pulled into a parking spot far away from them, and Stacey started to unbuckle her seat belt. I wasn't ready to get out just yet. I wanted that gold Cadillac Deville to be long gone first before I did.

"Stacey," I said, grabbing her hand and thinking of words to say fast at the same time. "I just wanted to thank you for letting me go to the doctor with you."

"You don't have to thank me, Ben." She said, trying to reach for the door.

I looked around again and found them still loading their car. Reaching for her, I said, "But you really didn't have to. The miracle of life is so amazing." I paused while watching them finish. I continued, "What can I do to thank you for sharing this moment with me?"

"Well, Ben, if the baby that I am carrying is yours, please don't abandon us." I quickly held her in an embrace to cover her face and to bury mine in her neck because the Caddy was rolling by slowly. I whispered in her ear, "No matter what happens between us, I could never abandon my child, and as I told you before, I am going to take care of what's mine. My child will not have a want for anything." I immediately let her go when I saw that the car was gone and out of sight.

"Thank you, Ben! I didn't know you cared so much." She said, and then kissed me on my lips gently.

I helped her out of the car, took her hand, and did not let go until we were inside of the store. I was walking around that store like I was the proud papa-to- be. I had shocked even myself. I couldn't help it. Just the thought of becoming a father was exciting. After she printed the wish list, we walked around the store to pick up the other items that weren't purchased. I was watching Stacey try to make up her mind between a denim blue or a mint green and light blue plaid diaper bag when my cell phone started to vibrate. I almost dropped it when I looked at the caller ID. I forgot I told Tamara to call me when her plane landed. I walked away from Stacey to take the call.

"Hey, baby, I see you got there safe and sound," I said, trying not to sound so nervous. I knew if Stacey found out who I was on the phone with, she would probably make a scene, just like she did when I told her it was over.

"Yeah, I did. What were you doing?"

"Nothing, baby. I'm out here doing a little shopping."
Please, Lord, don't let Baby's World blast one of their commercials right now. Before I could get the prayer out good, all I could hear was, 'Here at Baby's World, blah blah.' I had to hurry up and say something.

"Hey, are you still there?" I heard her say.

"Yeah, I'm here. My earbud came out, so if you said something, I missed it." I lied. I pressed the mute button so she couldn't hear that commercial.

"I miss you already," I told her.

"Aww, how sweet of you."

"Well, you know, I'm just that type of guy."

"Un-huh, well, guy...what are you buying for me?"

"You name it, and I got you."

"I love those words."

"I just bet you do," I said, looking around for Stacey, but I didn't see her. So I walked further away from where we were initially.

"Anything I want, huh?" She asked.

"Just about."

"What happened to name it?"

"That was before I thought about you and your girlfriends going shopping this weekend."

"You still could buy me something. You don't seem to mind me shopping at Adore Me. Especially when it involves something sexy to wear and that perfume that you are so crazy about."

"Keep talking like that, and I will be on the next flight out."

"Didn't you get enough this morning?"

"Girl, I can never get enough of you."

"You know, caramel is one of my weaknesses." She told me.

She had me going. I had an instant flashback to this morning. I couldn't wait for her to get home.

"I hope you know while you are doing all of this talking, you will have to back all this up."

"I would never...ever say anything that I couldn't back up." She said Seductively, with a sexy giggle on the tail end.

"I'm about to hang up before you make me gas up and drive to Baton Rouge."

"Bye, Ben. You are so silly."

"Woman, I'm not playing with you. You think I'm playing. Alright now. Don't say nothing when you hear the doorbell, and it's me on the other end. I'll just be waiting for you to answer so I can snatch your sexy ass off to a hotel somewhere. Don't doubt me now because I will-"

Stacey tapped me on my shoulder.

"You would what? What were you about to say?"

"Ah, we'll finish this conversation later. Let me finish handling this business, and I will call you in an hour, or so."

"Un-huh, if you can't stand the heat, stay out of the kitchen, baby."

"Girl, don't be startin' no mess you know you aren't prepared to handle," I said to both, Tamara and Stacey.

Stacey couldn't do anything but stand there with her arms folded with her lips in a pout.
"Ben, I will talk to you later, and we will finish this discussion."

"As long as you know that, you have been warned." I turned away from Stacey before she could say anything.

"Love you, baby."

"Love you, too, sweetheart. Bye." I hung up and turned back around to face Stacey, who was now beet red.

Seeing Stacey this way reminded me of the time she and I visited New York together. Stacey thought the desk clerk was being too flirtatious, but she really wasn't. Stacey turned this same color, but the only difference between now and then, she was trying to make me forget about any other woman existed. Now, she does not have a prayer.

Stacey was a very beautiful woman. She was a curvy little red-bone with long black hair. Even though she was pregnant, she was still fine. When it came time to holding her own, the girl was bad. She knew how to use what she had to get exactly what she wanted. But that was yesteryear.

Looking at her, I asked, "Is everything alright? You look upset." As if I didn't already know. Here we go with her hands on those bowed hips.

"Nothing is wrong when you and a man walk in a doggone baby store hand in hand...is overheard by countless people...talking about sleeping with someone else over the phone. Do you know this lady actually came up to me, and put her arm around my shoulders, and said,

"Ma'am, you can do much better than him. You poor, poor thing. **How embarrassing!?**"

"Kind of like this?"

She was talking too loud. Which aggravated the hell out of me. I am a grown man. My mother didn't even yell at me, and I was about to put Stacey in check.

"First of all, you are not going to loud talk me in this store," I said to her. "Secondly, I wa-" I know she just didn't walk off from me. Two can play at this game. "I was on the phone with my wife. Who cares what they think while they are passing judgment?" I asked, walking behind her, talking just as loud as she had been. I knew it was childish, but if she could dish it, then she should be able to take it. That fixed her butt.

I was tired. I was lying to my wife, and she wanted to front me over some craziness that really didn't matter. Those people didn't know us. Why should she care anyway? I guess I must have struck a nerve because she's standing here crying.

"Stacey, look, it's been a very long morning. I apologize for upsetting you, but you must understand the strain I am under, too." At this point, guilt was setting in, so I gave in and hugged her from behind.

"Stacey, I realize this isn't easy for you either, and it was insensitive of me, but I had to take the call. You can understand that, can't you?"

I apologized again. She finally stopped crying long enough to hear what I had to say. A woman and her friend walked by and chimed in by this time.

"Hmmph, girl...don't be so quick to forgive him. He was going to be with the other chick, anyway."

"They all do that." The other one said.

"Un-huh. That's why we put their asses on C. S."

They were going back and forth like this was some ghetto commentary segment entitled 'How to Get Over on your Baby Daddy Show.'

"Child Support?" Stacey asked her.

"You got that right. He won't leave me and go be somebody else without children. But then again, these dudes are so sorry out here, they'd go lay up with someone who had five kids for the help. What's an extra mouth to her?"

"And he should be helping her, not the other way around. But look, he might go to be with somebody else, but I'mma make sure, half his check stays right here with me. I ain't playing with none of them. I didn't make them by myself and I ain't finna care for them by myself."

All I could do was watch them in amazement. Stacey laughed her butt off like this was some big joke. These women didn't know us. They didn't know Stacey was only a sneaky link who was engaged to my brother. That she tried to ruin my wedding by telling my wife, the day before our wedding, that she was pregnant with my child, and it very well might not be true. They didn't know that I was going for be the best father to my son. They didn't know he wouldn't have a want for anything. They didn't know I was going to seek full custody of my son so that Tamara and I could raise him together. No, they didn't know any of that. But if I had said these things aloud, I'd be an asshole.

"I know that's right. That's survival of the fittest 101," Stacey said.

"You got it, girl. You are going to be alright."

"Looks like you got a good one. He looks like he works at the bank or something?" They started to laugh again. This time, they added high fives. I had had enough. My head was beginning to hurt.

"Are you ready to go?" I asked, interrupting their gathering.

The women moved on, still laughing and talking amongst themselves.

"Whenever you are." She said cheerfully.

"Good, let's checkout, and by the way, don't think you are going to use my child as a pun either," I told her.

"Whatever. I don't appreciate being disrespected, either."

"Disrespected!? Stacey, that was my wife on the phone. You were just a sneaky link! Besides, this child may not even be mine!"

I know the two women heard me because they were looking over in our direction. I heard one of them say, "Ooh girl, scandalous. Ole girl gets around, doesn't she?" They started to laugh again as they walked away.

Stacey had the nerve to stand there and be shocked. She looked at me with hurt in her eyes.

"You've done some low-down things to me, but this has to be the lowest of them all." She said, talking through her teeth with a menacing frown. "I hate the day I ever met you, and I hope that you are not the father of my baby. To think I ever wanted you to be his father. But I will tell you this, Benjamin Harris. If I never ever see your face again, I would be thrilled. You have humiliated me for the last time." She said, trying to force back her tears.

"But what if the baby is mine?"

"Don't worry, we'll get along without you. I will make it on my own just fine."

"How can you say that?"

"The same way you have said and treated me like your whore." She was livid.

"Stacey, I didn't say-"

"I really don't care right now...all I want to do is go home."

"Okay, I can see to you getting back home."

"Uh-uh, no, thank you. Don't do me any freakin' favors. You have done enough for me...today."

"I understand that you are upset with me right now, but the best thing for you to do is to calm down."

"Don't tell me to calm down. I don't need you to pretend to care for me now. **Forget you!**"

"Stacey, all this aggravation is not good for the baby, remember? So how about this? There are some rocking chairs over there next to the bathroom. Why don't you go and have a sit? I will pay for this and take you straight home, I promise."

"I can buy my own baby things. I don't need your help."

"I know you don't need me, but allow me to purchase these things. Didn't you tell me that you lost your job earlier?"

"So!?" She said, aggravated.

"So, why not let me do this for you?"

"I have more than enough money saved. I can afford to buy this. Besides, shouldn't you be worried that your precious wife will find out that you're spending your money on my baby?"

"Let me worry about that."

"Un-huh, let you worry about that. Well, who is going to worry if he is yours, and she tells you she doesn't want you to have anything to do with us, huh? What are you going to do then?"

I had to admit she asked a question I never gave thought to. What if?

"Stacey, I told you before. If this baby is mine, nothing and no one will keep me away from my child. Whether it's you or her, and I meant that."

"You say that now, but time will tell."

"It sure will." I will never forget this moment. I was putting my child before everyone, including myself. "So, do you have a name picked out for him?" I asked, rubbing her belly while she was calming down.

"Almost. Why? Do you have any suggestions?"

"How about Charles? We could call him Chuck for short." I suggested.

"Are you crazy? I am not naming my baby no Charles or Chuck."

"Your baby? He may be mine, too. Besides, I thought your family liked names starting with C's?"

"We do. That's why I thought about Cameron as a first name."

"I like that. It's a solid first name. What about the middle and last name?"

"We can name our son Cameron Benjamin Harris if you like?" She asked.

"I love that name. Thank you. Hear me out before you turn me away. I know it won't be easy, but I will be there...for you and for him."

"Do you really mean that for real?"

"Yes, for real. Until I know something different, this is my child, and I'm sorry for ever making you feel anything less than the beautiful woman that you are."

"That's all I needed to hear from you." She kissed me on my lips, and I felt nothing but gratitude from her.

"Now that we are parents again, can you take me to Dreamy's for a sweet treat? I want a strawberry pastry."

"Do you think that's a good idea?" I asked, pushing the buggy toward the front to checkout.

"What do you mean, a good idea?"

"Nothing. I'm trying to look out for you."

"Are you calling me fat?"

"Uh-uh, all I'm saying is, I'm trying to look out for you. How about some fruit or something?"

"I know you're not. I have you to know that I'm still fine, and will be finer when I get my flat stomach back. This baby has plumped me up in areas for free that some chicks have paid thousands for. You can't tell me nothing. I know I look good. You see it. I caught you checking me out earlier, Papi."

I can't lie. I was checking her out, but I'm not going to comment on my findings. All I'm going to do is smile and remember the fact that I love my life with my wife. Never mind how wider Stacey's hips have gotten and how the added weight complimented her so well in all the right places.

Yesterday was just wonderful. I thought as I looked at everything Ben had purchased. I couldn't wait to show them off. My shower was going to be held here at my townhouse. I couldn't wait. All I needed now was decorations, food, and guests. Jasmine should be here soon. I know she was waiting for TJ's girlfriend to come and pick up JJ for the weekend. She didn't like her because she felt like Erica took TJ from her, but that's not true. One thing I know for sure is that Erica is very loving with JJ. I thought Jazzy was going to kill somebody when he said he had two mommies. That little boy loves himself some Erica. I only want what's best for my child. If this is Ben's baby, I hope he, Tamara, and I can have a good co-parenting relationship. Hearing my front door open brought me out of my wishful thinking.

"Jazzy, is that you?"

"Yeah, it's me."

"What's wrong with you?"

"Nothing but tired. I need to start taking some iron. It just hit me all of a sudden, and I was so glad when Erica came and got that little boy. He was jumping up and down to hear she was on her way. He doesn't get that excited about his own daddy."

"Just be glad he loves her so much."

"Hmmph."

"What does that mean?"

"Nothing. You'll see when your little one comes. Anyway, let's get out the decorations because everyone else should be on their way with the food. The sooner we get everything out, the faster we both can go lay down. I got the balloons in my truck."

It took us thirty minutes to decorate. I was glad it wasn't much to do because I was tired. After we finished, Jasmine and I both took an hour nap. I was refreshed and ready to go when I woke up. I had dreamt of how yesterday started out so rough, and then it ended like a fairytale. I quickly showered and laid out my denim romper with a powder blue t-shirt to wear underneath. It was all about comfort for me. Since I've been pregnant, my hair has become thicker and longer, which I loved. I just hope it stays that way.

I wasn't going to do too much with my hair, so I decided to pull it back in a smooth ponytail and curl the ends with the hot curlers. My hair and outfit were on point. Looking in the mirror from the chest up, I could have been a cheerleader. I was taking one last look when both the doorbell and my cell phone started ringing at the same time. I grabbed my cell and answered it as I walked to the front door.

"Coming!" I yelled at the door.

"Hello?"

"Hey, I was calling to give my best wishes before your shower." He said as I was walking to answer the front door.

"Hold on a sec." Just as I thought, nobody but Big Mama. She was the first to arrive at everything.

"Come on in, Big Mama, and have a seat."

"Girl, it took you long enough, and don't close that door. Your aunt is right behind me. She has her hands full of stuff."

Big Mama came in holding nothing but her pocketbook. If she was so concerned about my aunt carrying a lot of stuff, wouldn't she think to help her? I kept that thought to myself and remembered that I had someone on the phone.

"Excuse me, Big Mama, I need to take this call, and I will be in the kitchen if you need anything."

"Un-huh, go ahead, baby. I'm in here now and I can do whatever I can to help."

"Yes, ma'am," I said slowly, not really sure what she was talking about because everything was done, but okay. "Hey, sorry about that," I said as I returned my attention back to my caller.

"Not a problem. I should have known you would be busy."

"Believe it or not, it really isn't at the moment."

"I hope you have a great shower. If you don't mind, I would like to come by."

"Really?"

"Yeah, if it is going to be a problem, then-"

"Oh, there's no problem," I said, cutting him off. I was just shocked he wanted to come over. "But I have to warn you. You will be the only man here in a house full of women."

"I don't mind if you don't." He said.

I was loving the attention I was being shown.

"Well, I'll see you later then."

"Is there something I can bring, or do you have everything you need?"

"After the shopping spree from yesterday, I don't really need anything but our baby."

"In due time." He said as we both laughed. See you in a bit."

I hung up the phone with the biggest smile on my face until I walked out of the kitchen and almost bumped into my aunt, who was staring at me like I stepped on her feet or something.

"What's wrong with you?" I asked her.

"Nothing. I've only been calling your name for the past five minutes, and you are standing up here grinnin' like some darn Cheshire cat." She said, rolling her eyes at me.

"Sorry, I didn't hear you." I told her.

"Un-huh, well, you got company."

"Oh." By the time I reached my living room, there wasn't anyone here that I would consider to be company. Company my foot. "I thought you said I had company, Aunt Carmen?" I asked her when she returned to the living room.

"Well, hello to you too, twin?" My sister said.

Now, I had an attitude because she was acting like I had some real guests. The only people that were here were my twin sister, Tracey,

Jasmine, her sister Keisha, and some other cousins.

"Your ungrateful behind should be glad that anyone is here at all."

"I don't recall inviting you." I snapped back.

"Excuse me, little girl?" She said, getting ready to stand up.

"Carmen, hush up that fuss! And I mean that. I can't remember
the last time when all of my granddaughters were all together in one
room. Look, Carmen, Tracey and Stacey really do lookalike, don't they?"

"Well, momma, they are identical twins."

"I know that, but Stacey was always so much smaller than Tracey.
Now that Stacey is pregnant. She's about the same size as Tracey."

"Un-huh," was all my aunt offered.

The only thing my sister and I had in common was that we looked
alike. But Tracey and I were as different as night and day, and I was
definitely the night. At times, my sister could be so stuck up.
Especially since she was a year away from having Dr. in the front of her
first name and M.D. behind the comma of her last. I, too, had a degree,
and she was no better than any of my Big Mama's 'grand-babies,' as she
called us. Because our parents paid for both our educations. She just
chose a different field than I had. She actually wanted to work, I didn't. As
little girls, our mother told us to work hard at whatever we wanted in life.
She said looks could only get us so far, but a good education could take us
wherever we wanted to go. I found it to be the opposite. My education
got me in the door, but my looks got me into some higher places.

My grandparents instilled that philosophy in our mother. They knew the value of having a good education. When Big Mama was younger, she moved from Puerto Rico to New York. There, she met the most charming black man she'd ever known. They would marry and become the proud parents of five children: three girls and two boys. Our mother was the baby. Moving to the South during those times wasn't easy. They raised their children, never to take an opportunity for granted.

All excelled, but one acted like the world owed her something. Aunt Carmen was the least of my favorite relatives. She always walked around like her stuff didn't stank, and my sister reminded me a lot of her. Aunt Carmen thought she was so much because she married a preacher, making her the First Lady of our home church.

She acted as if she was perfect, and her children could do no wrong. Some PK kids could get into the worst trouble. Keisha and Jasmine could cause so much drama Monday through Wednesday and raise hell Thursday through Saturday, but they would be the first to greet Deacon Rogers, who opened the church up on Sunday.

Especially that Keisha. She had to be in the spotlight, only to take her rightful seat next to her mama, wearing some big ugly hat. Keisha got pregnant by two different guys nine months apart, and Aunt Carmen had the nerve to talk about me becoming pregnant. I love my cousins, but their mammy was something else. That's why I don't take any mess off of her.

Aunt Carmen would always put our mama down for some reason

or another. I simply think it's because she was jealous of her. As my aunts and uncles came of age, they were given the choice of school or the military. There weren't any excuses given nor any accepted when it came to getting an education. She was married and out of the house when my mother became pregnant at nineteen with us. My mother never told them, not even us, who our father was. I remember when I was nine, and I heard my aunt lying on my mother, calling her all kinds of names.

She called my mother a dumb whore because she got pregnant by a guy and didn't know where he was. As a result, leaving her to fend for herself and two children she could not take care of. But Big Mama and Papi had my mother's back, and she hated it.

All we were ever told about our father was that he loved us very much and that he was too far away for us to see him. As I got older, I put two and two together and figured out that our father was married. He may not have been in our lives directly, but somehow, he was able to send our mother money every two weeks, and to this day, our mom sends us birthday and Christmas cards from him.

My mother didn't have to worry about anything. She got married when we were eleven, and both my sister and I were her flower girls. It was the most beautiful wedding I ever attended. We accepted our stepfather as being our dad, and everything was as good as life would have it for my family. Both of my parents were dentists and had their own practice. Aunt Carmen had a real problem with that. To her, my mother had it way too easy. Especially if you didn't come by it the hard way like she had, and my twin is the same way. I was like my mother, and Tracey was like the old bitter bat we called Aunt Carmen.

"Stacey, is your mother coming? Everybody is here except her and Cynt."

I looked at her like she was crazy because Tracey was sitting right next to her. Couldn't she have asked her that? Aunt Cynthia was my favorite aunt. Before I could answer the witch, Big Mama cut in.

"Carmen, you know that I told you that your sisters and their husbands went on that two-week cruise and won't be back until next Tuesday." Big Mama was becoming annoyed. She hated it when Aunt Carmen picked with people for no reason.

"Mmmph. I never would have put some little cruise before my daughter's shower. I hope she won't be out of the country when you deliver. That's just sad. Missing your first grandbaby's shower. Couldn't be me. Just pitiful, and who is running their business while they're doing all this extravagant traveling?"

Oh no, this helfa didn't. "Well, Aunt Carmen, it's unfortunate that our mother won't be here. But I'm just glad that you never missed your daughters' three baby showers back to back."

That shut her fat mouth up, and everyone laughed but her and Keisha.

"Mama, do you want something to eat or drink? How about you, Big Mama?" Jasmine asked her, trying to stop her from saying anything else.

"No, thank you." She replied through her teeth while staring at me.

"Well, I'll have some punch. I don't want to eat anything until her guest comes." Big Mama said.

"Oh, Mama, you don't have to worry about that. She ain't got no friends. Probably because they thought she might end up sleeping with their boyfriends or something."

That was it. That was the last straw. "No, that's not true. I don't have a lot of female friends because some chicks can be envious and bitter like yourself. Let's get something else straight right now while it's still family up in here." I said, sitting straight up. "You will not disrespect my mother, my son, or me in my house, and if you can't get with that program, **get up, get your ish, and get the hell out of my house while you still can!"**

"Stacey!" They yelled in unison.

But I didn't care. Jasmine put her hand on my shoulder as a sign to calm down and shut up. Because at this point, she had pissed me off and there was no turning back.

"Mama, why you have to start mess all the time?" Jasmine asked. "I know y'all don't know this, but Stacey can't afford to be upset, and that's all you are doing and for no good reason."

"Why are you taking up for her, Jazzy? She just about cussed our mama out, and I don't appreciate it, pregnant or not." Keisha said, trying to stand her fat butt up in those too-little jeans.

By the time she got up, I was already standing up and almost in her face.

"Like you gonna do something," I said. She had better be glad Jasmine was holding one arm and Tracey was holding the other.

"You need to be quiet, too, Keisha, and sit down," Jasmine told her sister.

Good thing she did as she was told before I knocked her big butt down.

"I'm just saying Jazzy, her sister ain't even taking up for her. Why should you?" Keisha asked.

"Because I understand the strain and stress she is under. Plus, I don't want her going into premature labor fooling around with y'all, and mama started all of this mess like she always does."

"Y'all are making me sick, disrespectful, helfas. Papa and I didn't raise any of you to disrespect their elders and talk like street women. Did you all forget that I was sitting here? Now, I don't want anybody to say anything else to upset this child, and I mean it. Carmen, don't you open your mouth no more to this girl. You always got something to say and always wondering why people treat you like they do."

"Mama, I don't mean no harm. I just wish that she could be more like her sister and stop depending on men to get ahead rather than herself. Your mother was lucky. You may not be. You won't stay pretty for forever. You better ask your mother. You see, she had to settle down and find y'all a daddy before it was too late."

"Let's just face some facts, Aunt Carmen. You are just jealous of my mother. You wished you could be her, don't you?"

"I'm not jealous of anyone. Unlike your mother, I know who my children's father is, and I have been happily married to him for over the past thirty years. What do I have to be jealous about? I am the First Lady of our church, and with all my duties, I don't have time to travel around the world chasing behind some man, drinking champagne, and wasting time like some folks do." She said, straightening her blazer as if it needed adjusting.

"Like I said, and now I know, you are jealous of our mother because you wished your life was as good as hers. My mother can't help that she got the looks, career, and the husband you wished you could have." I said, laughing at her.

No offense to Uncle Richard. He was the greatest, but she needed to be stopped.

"No, it's like I said. I'm not jealous of anybody. Besides, if it weren't for our parents, she wouldn't have the career she has now. They should have done to her like they did Charles, Chandler, Cynthia, and myself. Maybe if they were as strict on Chantil as they were on us, maybe she would have gotten pregnant by her husband, and not before."

"Are you trying to say that we didn't raise our child, right?" Big Mama asked.

"No, ma'am, I'm not saying that at all, but you must admit, you and daddy were much harder on us than Chantil. I believe that's what happened when she went off to that big school and came back home pregnant... just wasted y'all hard-earned money, yes she did." She said as if she had all the facts.

She forgot to mention that because of my mother, my grandparents were able to move into a beautiful four-bedroom brick home that looked better than hers.

"Well, let me ask you this, Carmen, since you seem to have all the darn answers. What happened with your two? I mean, both are unwed, and there are three babies between them. So, what poor parenting skills did you and Richard use? Because my baby girl graduated from college, got married, and both of their children have their college degrees. Your two hadn't even filled out a job application, yet alone gone to anyone's college. Now, for the last time, quit while you are ahead. As you can see, it's no fun when grown folks talk under your clothes. Now is it?"

I knew Big Mama was upset when she called out Aunt Carmen. When our grandmother became angry, she would speak in Spanish, and she was reading Aunt Carmen up one side and down the other. Aunt Carmen stepped outside the role of mother and child, and had to be put back in her place, woman to woman.

Now, she was just sitting there looking washed up and crazy.

"Some folks just need to get it together." She mumbled while rolling her eyes.

"Look, someone is coming. Let's end this discussion now. Twin come with me. I want to talk to you privately. Jasmine, you go and greet the guest. Big Mama, put on your biggest smile, and Aunt Carmen?"

"Yes, dear?" She said with a condescending flare.

"Please leave well enough alone. I heard what you said, and I don't agree with it one bit."

We were all surprised. She took over in a matter of minutes. We weren't used to Tracey saying anything. We had arguments all the time. She would shake her head and leave. I knew she didn't care about the drama and didn't come around our family because of it.

Pulling me into my bedroom and slamming the door behind us, she asks, "Twin, why didn't you tell me you were having complications?"

I couldn't help but drop my head because I knew that look from her all too well.

"You have your own life, and I didn't want to be a bother." Which was partly true.

"Why is it then, Jasmine knows more about you and my nephew than I do?"

Here we go again with this, you and Jasmine always leaving me out of stuff, mess.

"Twin, you know it ain't like that. Besides...she's always around, and you know how you get sometimes."

"How do I get sometimes? This is important, Stacey. Your health, the baby, all of it."

Tracey had always been jealous of my relationship with Jasmine.

"I'm sorry, okay. I will let you know if anything else should happen to us."

"Does mom know?"

"Well...no." I admitted

"Stacey! You haven't told mom either?" She asked, taken aback.

"Wait...before you fly off the handle, let me explain something. I just started having problems a month or so ago, and it was because of stress. Getting fired from my job has not been a great experience for me."

"**Oh, my God!** Now what? How are you going to make it? What is the father going to do to help? Where is he now? He should be here, too. Stacey, do you know how hard this is going to be for both of you? Oh, my God." She asked in a panic.

"See what I mean. You haven't given me a single chance to answer. Calm down. Trust me. I have everything I need, and then some. I have enough to be off for a while, and as far as my baby's daddy is concerned, well, we are working things out."

"Working things out? What is that supposed to mean? Are the two of you even together?"

"The question is, were we ever?" I had to laugh at that myself, but of course she didn't find it funny.

"Stacey, there is nothing funny about this. I just hope he is going to stick by you and the baby." She said, folding her arms.

"Tracey, why are you so negative?" I asked her. She was getting on my nerves. That's why I didn't like to tell her nothing.

"Because I wish you would make better choices in life."

"I'm not you!" I yelled.

"And I'm not you either, but still!" She yelled back.

"We aren't doing anything, Tracey, but going in circles. If you want, we can talk about this later, okay?" I was tired and had had enough.

"Fine, but you just remember this, you aren't alone anymore." She said, rubbing my belly. "That means you must do what's best for my nephew."

"Everything I do is for him. So don't worry, we'll be fine. Trust me." I understood where Tracey was coming from. I didn't need her preaching to me about taking care of my child. I heard enough of that coming from Aunt Carmen.

Everything turned out so nice. I had more clothes for my little pumpkin than I knew what to do with. Big Mama, Aunt Carmen, and Keisha were the first to leave. Which didn't make me any, never mind, 'cause my aunt didn't really want to be there, anyway. And Ms. Keisha will be crawling back with her tail stuck between her legs, apologizing like she always does. I don't understand why she even bothers or why we even bother to listen. It was good to see my old co- workers from the bank, Lisa and Crystal. The only two I had invited. I really liked them, and could count on them for the latest office gossip.

I waved goodbye to Lisa and Crystal as they walked to their cars. Walking up towards me was the biggest light brown teddy bear I'd ever seen, and behind it was the sweetest smile.

"I thought you weren't coming." I told him.

"I told you I would be here. I had a hard time finding the perfect gift." He said, holding the big teddy bear tightly.

"I don't know if this will fit through the front door," I told him.

"It better. It took me thirty minutes to get this thing in my car and ten to get it out."

"What made you buy this? It's cute, but dang." I said, laughing.

"Well, after the shopping spree you had for the baby yesterday, I figured you didn't have this, so here I am," He said, leaning over to kiss me on the lips.

"See, that's how you got knocked up in the first place," Jasmine said, causing everyone to laugh.

Laughing, I said, "Everyone, this is Terrance. Terrance, this is my family. My twin sister Tracey, and you know nosey Jasmine, and these are my other cousins."

"Hello, everybody. Wow, I didn't know you had a twin, Stacey. She is just as pretty as you are." He said with a big smile.

"She takes her looks after me. I'm the oldest between the two of us." Tracey said, smiling.

"Girl-bye, it was only by three minutes."

"It's a good thing that you're not having twins since you are a twin. I don't know." He said, looking at my belly. "Where do you want me to put this bear?"

"I can think of a few places, but you can put the bear into the baby's room."

He followed me in my baby blue painted room with teddy bear trimmed border.

"Baby, you've done a great job. It's nice in here. And guess what? I found the perfect spot to place the bear." He placed the teddy bear in the corner by the window.

I had to make a mental note of that because if I walked past this room too fast, I would mistake it for a six-foot-tall man. But it's cute, and it matched the border. I stepped back and took everything in, and I was so proud of my baby's first room. I must have been standing there for a while because I looked over and noticed Terrance standing on the opposite side of the room, watching me and smiling.

"What?" I said, smiling.

"You."

"Me. What about me?"

"Everything." He walked over, stood before me, and held both my hands.

"I don't know how, but I plan to be in my son's life if it kills me. I know this was a bad situation for both of us, and I'm sorry that I couldn't be there for you when you needed me the most. But believe me when I say I wanted to be here for you."

"I understand, Terrance, and I know that you tried. I'm sorry we had to be put in this situation to begin with. Do you know who ratted us out?"

"Nah, and if I did, it's nothing that I could do to them because they went directly to HR about our relationship."

"Well, you are here now, and that's all that matters." He leaned down and kissed me passionately, and I wished at that time that everyone was gone. The last 89time we were together was about two months ago. I couldn't wait to make up for lost time. But it would have to wait. I was too big and too tired to be fooling around.

"If you keep kissing me like this, we will have to put everybody out because you know how loud you can get." He said.

"Shut up, and just kiss me." Turning his baseball cap to the back, he was preparing for the long haul. Our kissing was interrupted by a loud commotion that was taking place in my living room. We broke our embrace, only to find all hell breaking loose.

"Where is that whore!?" The woman said, shouting.

"Who are you, and what are you talking about?" Jasmine asked her. "Do you have the right house?"

"You know doggone well who I am talking about. Stacey Johnson. Where is she, 'cause wherever she is, my husband is there too?" The lady stood at the front door with her arms crossed, mouth in a pout, and a stance that said she wasn't going to leave until she got what she came there for.

"Did someone call my name?" I said, walking past Tracey, who was now holding her hand up to her mouth in total disbelief.

"Yeah, I did. Do you answer to whore or just Stacey? Because if you ask me, they are one and the same."

"And you are?" I asked the woman.

"I am the wife of the man you have been sleeping with, and I know he's here because his car is out front. So, Terrance, you can bring your cheating behind out here, too. I want you both to hear this at the same time." She demanded, but Terrance didn't show.

"Lady, I don't know who you are and why you are here, but you need to leave," Jasmine said.

"I'm not going anywhere until I have my say. Terrance, you might as well stay in your whore's house because we are getting a divorce. And to prove it to you, your clothes are all over her front yard, and you will be served first thing Monday morning. And as for your bastard child, I hope you have found a good job because Terrance won't have enough money left to pay attention, yet alone to buy a postage stamp, especially after I'm done with him. Oh yeah, just so you know, I was the one who had you fired whore." That was the last thing she said before I slapped the cowboy spit out of her.

She fell back on the sidewalk, and I was trying to finish what I had started when I felt a cramp in my stomach. By the time I made it back into the house to sit down, Terrance was outside, fussing and fighting with his wife, Elise. How embarrassing? All of his clothes were everywhere, plus it had rained the night before, and some of his suits were in a puddle of mud.

Now, the police were outside about to take Terrance off to jail for domestic violence when it was she who was hitting him. She was the one who came to my house, disturbing the peace. He had done nothing wrong. Then the witch was trying to have me arrested, too, saying I had jumped on her. It was all I could do not to slap her again, but the pain that I was in had me barreled over.

I was having contractions and needed to be rushed to the hospital. I thank God for my sister and Jasmine. If it weren't for them, I'm not sure what I would've done. I'm just praying nothing is wrong with my baby.

Chapter 15

TAMARA

Monday morning came around fast since I came home Sunday night only to find my husband heading out on a business trip. I didn't mind that much. I knew H & G were working on a large merger. I just wished I had an opportunity to talk to him about my concerns about him being the father of Stacey's baby. But I guess I'll get that chance when he returns. I promised myself that I wasn't going to keep dwelling on the thoughts of him being unfaithful because I, too, had been. But the difference is I'm not pregnant, and she is. I needed to do something other than being stuck on I-65 in a traffic jam.

Everybody and their mama, including me, were headed downtown. Eight o'clock morning traffic was the worst. I'm kicking myself because I could have easily taken one of the side streets. If it hadn't been for me falling in my car this morning because Ben decided to drive it over the weekend, I would have been where I needed to go ten minutes ago. When he gets back, we are going to have a serious discussion about him using my car and not readjusting my seat. I looked over at the passenger side and noticed it, too, was leaning back. I had to call him because this was too much. I was getting ready to push his name, but I had an incoming call. Looking at the screen's caller ID, I knew this had to be good for Lisa to be calling this early in the morning.

"Hey, Lisa! What's going on?"

"Gurrrl, everything!" We both laughed.

"I said to myself, I knew this was going to be good for you to call this early in the morning."

"You better believe it is. Did I catch you at a bad time?"

"Only if you consider being stuck in a traffic jam on the freeway a bad time, then your answer is yes."

"That's what you get for not watching the morning news, and I bet you are not listening to the radio, either."

"Chile, you already know. When I was punching a clock, I watched and listened faithfully. Now, unless there's a meeting, it really doesn't matter. Besides, all they do now is talk on those radio morning shows. I like listening to music."

"I don't know why we are even having this discussion. I have told you a billion times that you should at least watch the morning news just in case there are some traffic problems or weather conditions you may need to be advised of. Now your non-punching clock butt is stuck on I-65 for the next twenty minutes. I guess you bought some sense, huh? Like my Madea always said, "Bought sense is the best sense, 'cause once you buy it, you'll never forget it."

"You know what I think about you, and your, I told you so."

"Yeah, but you and I both know I'm always right. Anyway, I know I told you this already, but the wedding was simply gorgeous. You were a beautiful bride, and most importantly, did you bring me something back?"

"Thank you for your compliment, and yes, I did. I don't know whose worst, you, mama, or Erica."

"We all are." She admitted.

"Shameful. Not one did you have a good time, or was everything good?"

"Knowing you, I already know everything was all good."

Little did she know that was far from the truth.

"You can give me all those gory details over lunch. I need to hurry-up and tell you this tea before someone comes in." She said.

"Oh, now I know this is going to be juicy."

"Guess where I was this Saturday?"

"I don't know. Where?"

"Stacey's baby shower!" Just hearing her name sent chills through my body.

"Gurl, you have not seen drama until you have been around Stacey and her family. I witnessed it firsthand. For starters, when Crystal and I arrived at Stacey's house, we heard arguing. I mean, they were loud, too. Crystal and I waited a few minutes before knocking. I was trying to hear what happened, but someone was speaking in Spanish. We stood there for the longest looking crazy. And when her cousin Jasmine answered the door, the tension was so thick, you could cut it with a knife."

"What was the argument about?"

"I'm not really sure. Something about someone being jealous of their mother or something. I never got all the details on that, but I did get a chance to see who Stacey's baby daddy was." If I weren't already sitting down, I would have needed to. I was not prepared to hear Lisa say my husband was at Stacey's house, but whether I wanted to hear it or not, she was going to tell me, so I braced myself. "And you know him," she continued. "Very well."

"How is that, Lisa?" Tears were forming in my eyes.

"Because it's Terrance!" She screamed.

"Wh-what did you say?"

"You heard me. **Terrance is the father!"**

"Girl, what!? How did you find this out?"

"Terrance showed up with the biggest teddy bear I'd ever seen."

"That doesn't mean anything, Lisa, he could have been just bringing a gift," I said, annoyed.

"Yeah, but his wife showed up after he did and took what appeared to be five trash bags out of her car. Honey, she flung that man's clothes, shoes, and drawls all over the front yard. It was a sight to behold, honey. Then she and Stacey got into it. Girl, Stacey slapped that woman so hard that she fell. That's when Terrance came outside, and he and his wife got into a physical altercation. She was pushing and hitting him because he was blocking her from hitting Stacey. Baby, he took every blow that woman gave him. Stacey had to be carried to the hospital by ambulance because she started having contractions."

"This is too much! Why did Stacey slap Elise?"

"Because she told Stacey that she was the reason behind her being fired."

"Fired!"

"You heard right! Apparently, she reported their affair to human resources."

"Girl shut up! Are you serious?"

"Serious as a heart attack. I heard her say she knew the baby was Terrance's and that Stacey could have his triflin' good for nothing and some other choice words."

"What?!"

"Then the police showed up, and that's when I decided to get ghost because I didn't want to be nobody's witness. They really didn't need me anyway because there were plenty of people standing outside that witnessed what went down."

"I can't believe the baby is Terrence's," I said aloud in astonishment and relief.

Lisa was still talking, but I had checked out. I didn't know what or how to feel. I didn't know if I should feel relieved or angry. Lisa broke my thoughts by calling my name.

"Tamara?"

"I'm sorry, Lisa. I guess I am still in shock."

"What's up with lunch today? Can you fit me in your schedule, boss lady?"

"I don't see why not, but let me check today's agenda on my

tablet."

She was still talking, and once again, I checked out. I was glad I had made it to work and parked because after hearing all of this, has definitely sent me on a whirlwind. I opened my console and saw a parking stub on top of my tablet. "Greater City Memorial Hospital." I read.

"Yeah, that's what I was saying."

"You were saying?"

"Yeah, are you not listening to me? I said that we all go to the same OB/GYN practice."

"We? I go to Dr. Daniels."

"Yes, silly we. Your Dr. Daniels formed a partnership with-,"

"Harpe and Morgan," I said, reading the back of the parking stub.

"That's right. Stacey is under Dr. Morgan. I heard she was really good, too."

"Un-huh," was all I could say. "Did Stacey have her baby?"

"Nope, the last I heard, it was a false alarm."

"Drama, drama, drama." I was pissed. Ben was keeping things from me again, and I wanted to know why. I had some questions that needed to be answered PDQ!

I was walking through my office door when I told Lisa I couldn't meet with her for lunch. I knew it was a lie, but I was in no mood for socializing. I told her if my plans changed, I would call her back, but I already knew that I wouldn't. Lisa and I are close friends, and one thing I know about her was she could tell if I was upset. She had no idea of the trouble Stacey had caused me, and although I would tell her about the whole ordeal, now was not the time.

Settled in my office with the door closed, I picked up the phone to call Ben, and he had better have some good answers. If not, a divorce may be in our near future.

Chapter 16

BENJAMIN

I had just stepped out of the shower when my cell rung. I started not to answer, but when I saw it was Tamara, I knew I had to.

"Hello Beautiful?"

"Did you drive my car while I was gone?" She asked, quickly.

"Well, hello to you too, and yes, I did. Why?" I asked, hoping no one had seen me.

"Because I almost broke my damn neck getting in the car this morning. You had my driver's seat pushed all the way back."

"Snickering, I said, "I'm sorry, baby. I meant to pull it up before leaving, and I forgot. I'm so sorry."

"It looks like you had company, too."

Now I knew someone had seen me.

"Yeah, I did," I said in a more serious tone.

I didn't know where this was going. All I knew was I didn't have thirty minutes to argue about it. I decided to let her say what she had to so I could be on time for my luncheon.

"Well?"

"Well, what?" I asked in return. "Well, who was it?"

"Is that important?"

"Yes! Unless you have something to hide..."

"I have nothing to hide. I just don't understand the reason for all these unnecessary questions. Is there something wrong with the car?" Knowing that it wasn't, I just wanted her to spit out what she had to say so that I could go.

"No, there's nothing wrong with my car, but I don't understand why in the hell you didn't tell me you had Stacey up in my car, joy-riding her ass around town."

"First of all, Tamara, I am going to say this, and I'm going to be through with it for now. I was wrong for not asking your permission to use your car. Secondly, Stacey asked me to take her to her doctor's appointment as you know. But I wanted to know how soon I could get a DNA test, and third, I was not joy riding her around in your car. Your car seemed to be more comfortable than mine, so I took yours." My patience had just run out. Either she was going to accept my apology, or she would just be upset until I could talk to her face to face.

"How dare you talk to me like I'm some child?"

I guess the apology was no longer an option.

"Tamara, this is silly. You are my wife. I was not trying to talk down to you. I just wanted you to hear what I was saying loud and clear."

"What I heard loud and clear is that the baby is not yours, so you can stop campaigning for the Father of the Year award."

"What do you mean? How did you find that out?"

"Just know I heard this from a reliable source."

"A reliable source? Tamara, I need proof, not some office gossip. I ain't buying it."

"What are you talking about? Unless you just want that baby to be yours, this should have been the best news you heard all day."

"Sta-, I mean Tamara...I'm sorry. I didn't mean that."

"No need. You just confirmed for me what it is you really want."

After saying that, she hung up. I had to be the biggest idiot on the face of the earth. I was trying to tell her that Stacey was not my concern. She was. I tried to call her back, but the call went directly to voicemail. I will give her some time to cool off and give her some space. I knew this was hard for her, but I needed her to know where I was coming from as well.

***

Chapter 17

TAMARA

I was visibly upset, but I wasn't crying or anything. I had had enough, and my facial expression told it all. I'll forgive Ben for almost calling me by Stacey's name, but what I had a hard time with was him purposely not telling me he had taken her to the doctor. I wouldn't have liked it, but I would have understood. He had made some valid points. I turned my phone off because I didn't want to argue with him anymore. I just wanted to be left alone. I needed some peace, time, and space. I didn't want anyone giving me 'if it were me' advice. Anyone could give an opinion, but unless it happened to him or her, they wouldn't know what I was going through. I was standing by my office window, looking out, when I heard a knock at my door.

"Come in." Who could this be?

"Hey, lady, I'm surprised to see you here today," he said, smiling.

"Yeah, here I am in the flesh," I said, flopping down in my seat.

"What's wrong with you?"

"Phillip, I wouldn't know where to start."

"Try the beginning." Phillip pulled out the chair in front of my desk and sat down.

"Well, for starters, I don't know if you knew this or not, but my husband thinks he has a baby on the way."

"Thinks?" He asked.

"Yeah, I heard the woman who calms she is having his baby is actually pregnant by someone else. My husband is too stupid to see that this woman is only trying to play him."

"Did you share this information with him?"

"Of course I did. But he dismissed it by saying it was mere office gossip." "In other words, he needed proof."

"Exactly."

"Have y'all discussed the possibility of it being true?"

"No," I answered.

I tried to explain to Phillip what had happened, from the letter the night before our wedding to the bad dreams I'd had. I couldn't stop my tears from falling. Phillip stood and walked around my desk, pulled me out of my executive chair, and held me close. I couldn't help but let go. I was finally feeling relief.

All I needed was someone to understand the pain I was feeling, and at that moment, Phillip had lent me his shoulder to cry on.

"I know you are hurting now," he said. "But you have to believe that everything will work out the way it should. I'm not going to stand here and say, 'Oh, everything will be better tomorrow,' because I don't know that to be true. But if you believe your husband loves you, and I have no doubt that he does, pull strength from the love you both share and move forward."

"It's hard, but I will try, Phillip."

"Good, because if crying solved anything, we all would be

swimming in an ocean of tears."

We both laughed.

I knew he was right, and I felt better. "Thank you for allowing me to cry on your shoulder."

"No problem. You never know when I may have to cry on yours."

"I doubt that very seriously." He kissed me on my forehead, and I walked him to the door. We said our goodbyes, and I returned to my desk to catch up on the minutes from the meetings I missed. Sometime after, I received flowers from Ben. His note read.

Your husband is an idiot. Please forgive him.

Love,

Ben

I had to admit the flowers were beautiful, and the card made me laugh. I called him and thanked him for the flowers. He had apologized again and promised never to keep, conceal, hide, or shelter anything else away from me.

I hated to see Tamara so upset. I knew about Ben and Stacey, but I didn't want her to know that I had. I wanted to know what her thoughts were. Truthfully, this situation is rather messed up. Who was I to tell anyone about holding on to what they have, when I for damn sure didn't know what to do about my own situation? It wasn't that I didn't love Kherington, but I wasn't in love with her and hadn't been for quite some time. We were basically just going through the motions.

In my case, no one wanted to be the first to say goodbye. It was good in the beginning, but as time passed, we fell into this pattern. No excitement, no spontaneity. We rarely had sex anymore. So why in the hell am I still in this relationship? Is the question that I mentally ask myself whenever I think about her. I've even asked Kherington. She said that it's because of our history that we are still together. History, huh? But what about now, the present? I had convinced myself that no matter what, I was going to end the madness soon. There was no need to keep holding on to something that wasn't healthy. It was time for me to move on. That's why I told Tamara that if she believed that their love for one another was strong, then they would make it through this. Love was no longer the bond that kept us together, and I needed to talk to Kherington before our relationship became even more toxic than it already was. I took out my cell and dialed her number.

"Dr. Drake."

"Hey, where are you?" I asked, hearing all the laughter and chatter in the background.

"I told you I had to attend a conference this week."

"That's right, you sure did. Um, when do you think you'll be back?"

"Why?"

"Why? Because I wanted to know. Look, I didn't call you to start an argument. I just wanted to know so we could sit down and talk."

"Talk about what, Phil? How many women you are sleeping with behind my back, or have you found your heart and decided you wanted a genuine commitment?"

"Why is it whenever I want to have a serious conversation, you always throw up junk from the past? Look, all I want to do is see you when you get back, if that's not too much to ask for."

"If you want to stop seeing me, fine. We don't need a long, drawn-out conversation to say it's over. Besides, I already know you don't love me, so why not just end it here and now?"

"Fine, have it your way. It's over. Have a wonderful life," I said and hung up. She would be calling back. I had no doubt about it. She always has. This time was going to be different. I was not going to sit around and listen to her crocodile tears. I have resigned from that position, and I must say, I feel unburdened.

My mind flashed back to Tamara. I was hoping that she was doing okay. It had been at least three hours since I saw her. I wondered if she was still here, so I tried to buzz her office, but got no response. I was about to call her when Kherington's phone number popped up. I sent her ass straight to voicemail and dialed Tamara's number.

"Hi, Phillip."

"Hey, Tamara. I was calling to check up on you. Are you feeling better?"

"Yeah, I am...but you know." She sighed. "I have my moments."

"Yeah, well, I have nothing to do, so would you like some company or my other shoulder to cry on?"

"I'm all out of tears, but your company sounds good."

"Have you heard from Ben yet?"

"He did the funniest thing. He sent me a bouquet of flowers with a note that read to forgive him because he was an idiot." We both laughed.

"Well, you got to give it to my boy. At least he is truthful. I am glad it made you laugh, and you're not so sad anymore. That's really good."

"So, what are we doing tonight?" She asked.

"I'm not so sure. I mean, we could go out to eat dinner or something."

"We'll hammer that out when you come by. What time should I expect you?"

"How about seven?"

"Seven it is. I'll see you then."

"Okay, bye."

I was loading up my stuff to go home when my cell rang. "Nobody but Kherington," I said aloud.

I answered, but I didn't say anything.

"What is it about me that you hate so much?"

"What in the hell are you talking about, Kherington?"

"I mean, you don't feel anything for me? All that we have been through, and you could...just...throw away our relationship like it was a useless rage doll." "Kherington," I said softly. "It hasn't been the same for us in a long time. We pretty much have been going through the motions." I could hear her crying in the background.

"I know, but at least I figured that we could try. My God, man, I gave up a lot for you."

"And I appreciate that, but we both know this relationship has been over for a while, especially since that time."

"Phillip, I can't believe you. Did you know, because of your selfishness that I...that I...," was all she could get out.

She didn't have to finish. I knew what she was about to say. I sat down in the chairs by my door. With a lump in my throat, it was my turn to speak.

"Kherington, I'm sorry, but you know, if I had to do it all over again, that it would have been different, knowing what I know now, but that outcome can't hold us hostage in this relationship. Why would you want to stay in a relationship with someone that you don't love just because you feel that they owe you something?"

"That's exactly how I feel. You owe me your life for the one I had to lose. **Because of you**," she shouted. "I had an abortion that I did not want. Now, I may never be able to conceive a child. Yes, I'll say you owe me. I may never know what it means to bring a child into this world."

"Kheri, you know it was not a good time in either of our lives. I was just starting out trying to get this company off the ground. I had no money for real. Everything we earned, we reinvested in the company, and what about you, huh? You were in your third year of med school. Were you willing to put your career on hold to raise a child? All you ever talked about was when you got your degree, you were going to do this and do that. It wasn't until a year ago that you found out that you may not be able to conceive. And since that time, our relationship has not been the same. Your feelings for me possibly changed at that time. Am I right?"

"Partially, but it didn't have to do with just that. I thought about how even after you were on your feet, and I was out of med school that you still hadn't committed to our relationship. That's when I decided why I should even bother, because you weren't going to settle down. You liked your lifestyle and weren't trying to change. You loved being a millionaire playboy."

"I know I owe you a lot. But I'm not ready to settle down, and I really don't know if I'll ever be. Are you willing to wait for me?" I asked, already knowing the answer.

"Hell no... and since you do owe me, make it at least a ten-carat, flawless diamond ring."

"Girl, please, you're a good woman and all, but you're not that good." "You damn right, I'm better. But I still want my carats. You can afford it, deep pockets." She said, laughing.

"Alright, woman, I got to go. So, when are you coming back?"

"I'm not telling you. Why do you want to know? So I won't catch you with another woman at your house."

"Nah, so you won't catch me with another woman at my house, but yours." "You bet not bring any other woman to my house-"

"Calm down, I was just playing, girl. Damn."

"Anyway, I may come home tomorrow...maybe?" She said.

"Whenever you do decide to come home, call me so that we can finish our conversation. Don't do nothing I wouldn't do." I told her.

"Too late, bye."

***

I looked at the clock on the wall. It read eight sixteen. I was having second thoughts about going over to Ben's house. Since Tamara and I danced in her office, I had developed feelings for her and I knew she could feel them as well. Despite how I felt, I couldn't allow my feelings to get in the way of my business and friendship with Ben. If I acted on them, I wouldn't just settle for being the other man. I had never been in that position and never planned on being. Seeing Tamara cry today did something to me. All I wanted to do was hold her and never let her go. It was getting late, and I had a choice to make. Either I was going, or I would call her to say otherwise. My heart said to go, but my mind said to stay. I had too much at stake. "Oh, what the hell," I said as I grabbed my keys and a bottle of wine. I didn't live too far from them, only a corner and a driveway away.

I pulled into their driveway and was looking at the front door. I made myself promise not to act on the feelings I had for her. I took a deep breath, got out of the car, walked up to the front door, and rang the doorbell.

"Who is it?" she asked.

"It's me, Phillip." She opened the door, looking good as usual. She turned around for me to follow her, wearing these fitted jeans. Mmm, I loved the way she walked. She was sexy for no reason.

"I thought you weren't coming."

"I had a minor setback, but I did bring you something." I held out the bottle of wine for her to see.

"I'll be right back with two wine glasses. Do you want something to eat?"

"No thanks, I'm good for now, but if you want, we could go grab something."

"No, I'm good, but I have some imported cheese and crackers that would go great with this wine."

"I'm willing to give that a try." I don't know why I'm acting so nervous.

I was looking around like I hadn't been here only a thousand times. She reentered the room with everything she had promised.

"Okay, Phillip, take your shoes off."

"Excuse me?"

She laughed.

"Take your shoes off. You are acting strange. I don't know if it's because of me or if you are uncomfortable being here."

"I'm sorry. I don't know why I am acting like this," I said, pulling off my shoes.

My heart rate was beating extremely fast, and I was starting to sweat.

"Are you okay?" She asked.

"It's a little warm. Do you think you could bring me some water?" I took my sweater off and felt better.

"Here you go."

"Thanks, I needed that. I hope I'm not coming down with anything. It just hit me."

"Me either. The last thing I need is you germing up my spot." She said, smiling.

"You got jokes."

She stood up, dimmed the lights, and put on some music. The selection she chose played the smoothest after-hour jazz. We decided to sit on the floor with our backs leaning against the sofa. I had to admit, it was a little too nice and cozy for my liking, and the wine didn't help any.

We sat there and laughed and talked for hours. I looked at my watch when I drank the last of my wine.

"You are not going to believe this, but it is two o'clock in the morning."

"Are you serious?"

"Yeah, see." I showed her my watch as I stole a glance at her beauty. "It has gotten late, and I need to be heading home," I said, getting up off the floor and then helping her up.

"Thank you for coming and lending me your ear." She said.

"Anytime, anytime you know that," I said, smiling at her as she walked me to the door.

"Wait, you are forgetting something." "What's that?"

"This." She held up my sweater.

"I would have remembered that when the cold air hit me."

"That you would have." She handed me my sweater, and I began to pull it over my head. "Let me help you with that. You seem to be having some trouble." She said.

"I can do it, Mommy, all by myself, see," I said in a baby voice. I pulled it down over my head.

"Un-huh, but let momma tell you a little secret." She used her index finger to motion for me to come closer. So I leaned forward. "It's on backwards." She said, whispering in my ear and then laughing.

"Whatever. If I turn it around, can I get a hug for doing a good job?"

"Yes, but you have to turn it around first, then I'll give you a hug
for being a big boy."

"Woman, I'm a grown-ass man. Give me my hug 'cause I'm finna
go." I reached around her waist and pulled her close to me. I gave her the
biggest hug I could offer. After hugging her, I released her, but she did not
me. She tilted her head and began to kiss me. Not thinking, I parted my
lips to taste the sweetness of the wine that lingered on her tongue. The
longer we kissed, the more I caressed her body. The more I caressed her
body, the harder I became. Moans escaped both of us. It was only until
my sweater had come off and I was unbuttoning her jeans that reality had
sat in. I grabbed her hands, which were busy unbuckling my belt.

"Tamara, we can't do this," I said, out of breath.

She kissed my neck.

"Phillip, you know you want this just as much as I do." She said,
rubbing up against me.

"If you keep doing that, you're right. It would be hard, and I do
mean hard, to walk away."

"So why walk away at all?"

"Because I know deep down, this is not what you want. It's the
wine that's causing you to act this way."

"I know what I want, and right now, it's you." She said, kissing my
lips. This time, I didn't part them.

"No, Tamara," I said, pulling away from her, grabbing my sweater, and backing up to the door. "I will not allow you to do this," I said and left. I could have kicked myself for coming over here. I knew it was a bad idea from the beginning.

Chapter 19

TAMARA

I didn't get an ounce of sleep last night. All I could do once Phillip left last night was sit there and think about what I had done. How could I have thrown myself at Phillip? How am I going to face him today? To say I'm embarrassed was an understatement. What is he going to think of me? I can't stay here all day. I'm going to have to face him, now or later. I may as well make it now. I got up, walked out of my office, and went right into his, closing the door behind me.

"Phillip, do you have a minute?"

"Sure."

"I just wanted to tell you how very, very sorry I am. I promise I will never drink again. It was foolish of me to act that way. Mainly because you've been such a good friend to me. I hope what I've done doesn't change that about us."

"There's nothing to apologize for, and don't worry, we will continue to be friends." He said dryly.

I didn't know how to take that, so I shook my head in agreement and turned around to leave.

"Tamara." He called.

I stopped walking when I heard my name. I turned around, and he walked over to me. He wrapped his arms around me and planted a kiss that I will never forget. This time, it was he that had taken the lead, and I gladly followed. We were going at it until we heard a knock at the door. I could not afford for anyone to find me sitting on Phillip's lap in a compromising position. I immediately jumped up and sat in a chair across from him, who was straightening his shirt.

"Come in." He said thirty seconds later.

"Good morning, guys. Here is your mail, Phillip and Tamara. I've already delivered yours. Is there anything I can get for anyone?" Ms. Hopkins asked with a smile.

"No thanks," I said.

"I'd like some water, please," Phillip said. As she was pouring Phillip's water, I decided to make a beeline for the door. I needed to get out of there fast. But who I hoped to avoid the most had just walked in.

Chapter 20

BENJAMIN

Tamara and I almost collided as she tried to leave Phillip's office.

"Good morning, everyone," I said, speaking.

"Good morning, Ben." Ms. Hopkins said.

I loved Ms. Hopkins. She always wore a smile. She used to be the secretary for our church until her husband took ill and passed away. Pop had always said she was the best secretary he ever had. So, when I thought the time was appropriate, I asked her to join our team, and she has been with us ever since.

"I laid your mail on your desk, Ben. Can I get you anything?"

"Yep, did you bring us any of your delicious blueberry muffins today?" "Like father, like son." She said with hands on her hips. "I'm going to tell you, like I used to tell him, lay off the muffins before you become too thick around your waist like me." She said, laughing.

"But I'm still young, Ms. Hopkins. I can still work mine off."

"Un-huh, yeah. That's what he said, too, but look at him now." We all laughed. "Well, since you all don't need anything, I will be at my desk." She said, leaving.

I was still holding Tamara around her waist.

"Good morning, beautiful," I said, leaning over to give her a kiss when she pulled away from me.

"What are you doing here?" She asked, like she was disappointed or something.

"Well, good morning to you, too." I gave her a quick kiss on the cheek, anyway. "What's up, boss man?" I said, walking over to give Phillip a pound.

"You got it, man."

Tamara went to sit down in one of the two chairs in front of Phillip's desk. "I'm glad both of you are here. I wanted to tell you about the deal in Dallas.

You guys have got to go visit the location. I am so excited about it, that I came here straight from the airport." I said, sitting across from Tamara and facing Phillip, who was sitting behind his desk.

"It sounds exciting. How soon can we go look at the site?" Tamara asked. "As soon as you'd like. All I need now is for Phillip to go look at the location and go over the numbers with you. But let me warn you. I got first dibs on that little black sports car on the showroom floor."

"Man, how are you going to call first dibs when I hadn't been there to see what they even carried?" Phillip asked.

"Too bad, dawg, you should've called shotgun on this one. I had a ball test driving everything they had."

"Sounds more like a pleasure trip than a business one," Tamara said, looking at me.

"I can't lie. I had a ball. So what have you two been up to since I've been gone?" I asked, unbuttoning my sports jacket and leaning back in the chair. No one said anything, but I did pick up on the exchange of looks that they gave one another.

"So what's up?" I asked sternly.

Phillip sighed before speaking.

"We might as well come clean, Tamara." She looked at him, then me, and turned her head. "You almost caught us-"

"Don't!" Tamara shouted.

"Don't what!" I said, standing to my feet.

"We almost got caught brainstorming about your Christmas present." He said. "Christmas present?" I asked, looking at Phillip.

"Christmas present." He repeated.

"Christmas present?" I looked at Tamara, searching her face for anything that said anything different.

"Christmas present." She said softly. Feeling relieved, I sat back down.

"Did you know that you're the hardest person to shop for?" He said, laughing.

"Really, I'm not. All you had to do is ask what a brotha wanted."

"What kind of surprise is that?" Tamara said, standing and laughing. "That's the point, it's not." I stood up and grabbed Tamara by the hand, pulled her to me, and whispered in her ear. "I have a big overdue present that I would love to give you when we get home. Tell Phillip goodbye."

"Bye, Phillip, and thank you for all of your help." She said as I was pulling her to the door.

"You're welcome anytime. If you have any time to spare, I would love to finish our conversation. We were really starting to get somewhere."

"I don't know, Phillip. It may not be necessary to finish. I believe I have all that I need."

"Phillip, my man, on that note, we'll talk about this deal more tomorrow."

"Sounds good. Take it easy."

"You know I will," I said as I walked my wife out the door.

***

Chapter 21

TAMARA

When Ben and I left Phillip's office, we went home to discuss this Stacey drama. Ben told me that he was going to seek full custody of the child if he was the father. I disagreed with him. Even though she was not one of my favorite people, I wouldn't want anyone to have their child stripped away from them. I believe a child should be with their mother unless she proved otherwise. Needless to say, that turned into an argument, one after another. We finally agreed to disagree about the whole situation and tried to avoid talking about it at all costs.

Today was no different. We were having Thanksgiving dinner at his parent's house. I had to give it to Mother Harris. She threw down on this dinner. We had ribs, honey-baked ham, fried turkey, and cornbread dressing with gravy. Our sides were macaroni and cheese, mashed potatoes, candied yams, collard greens, string beans, and cranberry sauce. She made three cakes for dessert: German Chocolate, Red Velvet, and a Sour Cream pound cake. Two pies, pecan, and sweet potato, and one peach cobbler. Mother Harris had cooked enough food to feed a nation. None of it would have gone to waste. They had family everywhere. I only wished Mama could have come, but I knew this was her busiest season. She had not forgotten about me, though. She sent me some of her famous yeast rolls.

It was a wonder that Erica and I had found somewhere to go with people being everywhere. We hid away in Ben's old bedroom with our phones, searching for the best Black Friday sales. Ben and the other men were in Pop's den downstairs or anywhere else they could find to watch the football games. Everyone else was spread throughout the house.

"What store do you want to look at first, Tamara?"

"Depends on who is opening the earliest."

"I'll take this store, and you take the other one."

We scanned those sales ads backward and forward. You would have thought we believed in Santa from the lists we had compiled.

"Do you know what you're going to buy for JJ?" I asked.

"Yeah, kind of. I know what I would like to give him, but I'm waiting to see what TJ does. I'm trying hard not to duplicate anything."

"I know my little cousins are crazy about these Barbie Dolls."

"Yeah, in a minute, we will find out if you're going to purchase toys yourself." Erica said.

"Don't remind me. For all I know, she could have had the baby by now. Ben hasn't told me anything."

"Well, TJ told me her baby was due on the 8th of next month, so girl, you have two weeks or so, for this nightmare to be over."

"Or to begin," I said. "It's a shame that I have to get all my info from a third party rather than Ben himself."

"Two weeks, Tam. Two weeks." "Lord, help me make it."

"He will. Watch and see."

My cell phone vibrated. I looked at the caller ID and saw it was

Ben calling me. I put him on speakerphone.

"Yes, Dear?"

"Where are you?"

"In the house with you."

"Where in the house?"

"In your old bedroom."

"By yourself?" I could hear the smile in his voice.

"No nosey. I'm here with Erica."

"Um, what are y'all doing up there?"

"You are full of questions, aren't ya?" I asked him.

"Hey, TJ, Tamara, and Erica are upstairs in my bedroom, dawg. You wanna go up?" He asked TJ.

"Ah, excuse you. But we hadn't said we wanted any company."

"Who is this...Erica?"

"Who else?"

"What are you doing on the phone?"

"You are on speakerphone."

"Speakerphone?"

"Yeah, so stay your horny butts down there."

"All I know is both of y'all are in one bedroom with two beds, so what's up?"

"You obviously, because we ain't getting down like that," I said.

"Tamara, how are you gonna leave me like this? I need your help to work off this food I just ate."

Erica and I laughed. "Man, get me off my phone. In your parent's home at that." I told him.

"Why are y'all trippin like this?"

"Bye, Ben," I said.

"Yeah, bye Ben, and tell ya homeboy, I said don't try it. It ain't happenin' here either." Erica said.

We hung up less than three minutes later. They both were at the bedroom door. It was a good thing we had locked it.

"Tamara, why are you trippin?"

"I'm not, and I'll get with you in two weeks," I said, talking to him through the bedroom door, referring to Stacey's due date.

"What's so special about two weeks?" He asked. But then I heard TJ mumble something. "Tamara, you can't be serious. I know we aren't going to do this today. Man, why you trippin?"

"You think this is something? Wait until December 9th. I'll really show you something." I said, giving Erica a high five.

"Man, I'm through with this," He said.

Apparently, he walked away because I heard TJ call his name.

"Tamara, I hope you know that you're hurting him," TJ said.

"Not as much as he has hurt me, TJ," I snapped back.

"How long are you going to punish him?"

Opening the door and glaring at TJ, "As long as it takes." Erica said.

TJ backed away without saying another word. She then closed the door and returned to her phone and shopping list.

"Do you want to talk about it?" I asked.

"Nope, let's get back to what we were doing."

"Fine by me. You know this is my favorite time of the year. What better time other than the holidays can I go therapy shopping, and everything I purchase is on sale? We need to leave now and take a two-hour nap. Do you think TJ will still let us get his Suburban?"

"Un-huh, we took separate cars over here. I wanted to make sure I could go on with the truck and not have to drop him off at home."

"Hey, we can sleep at Lisa's house since she lives closest to the mall."

"You know what? We should have been doing this the entire time."

I called Lisa to make sure she didn't have any company coming over. Erica and I didn't want to interrupt anything if she had. It turned out that she and her guy friend were having dinner over at his parent's house, and would meet us at her place later.

Before leaving, I called Ben to tell him I was leaving, but he didn't answer his phone, and when I looked for him, he had already left with TJ. So I guess we were back to not speaking to each other again.

Chapter 22

TAMARA

Either my husband was the dumbest man on earth, or he was just too trusting. He sent me away with Phillip. Phillip and I took the company's private jet to Dallas. We both had our work cut out for us. I was there to review the numbers, and Phillip was there scouting the area for profitable growth, so he said.

When our plane touched down, I was already tired. Ben and I weren't on speaking terms, and I didn't really have the energy to fight with him anymore. So whatever he said about his situation, I let it go at that. I talked to Erica and Phillip about it. They both were saying the same things. I should not give up if my marriage meant what it did to me.

After we toured the site and Phillip drove around in all the cars he wanted, I requested to go back to the hotel.

"If you have finished playing, can we go?"

"Playing, girl, you don't get any better than this." He said, pointing at the cars he had just driven.

"I am hungry and tired. Unless you are about to purchase something, let's go."

"Before we go, you have got to let me drive you around in this." He said, pointing at a 2025 Maserati GT. It was sleek and sexy, just the way I liked it.

Phillip wanted to go out to dinner, but as tired as I was, dinner would have to come to me. I told Phillip we could have dinner in my room around seven. It was a quarter till when my phone rang. It was Ben, and I was in no mood to argue.

"Why didn't you call to let me know you had arrived safely?" He barked. "Look, I hadn't had time to call anybody. As soon as the plane landed, a car picked us up, and we had been on a tour. I'm not out here playing around. Unlike you when you were here last, and now Phillip."

"Baby, we can't help it. Those cars, man, ooh. Did you see my car?"

"I have some bad news."

"Bad news. What's that?"

"Well, the car you wanted isn't here anymore."

"What do you mean? What happened to my car?"

"Well, it sorta wasn't your car from the beginning. The car had already been sold before you arrived. They were so excited to see you and to show you around that they forgot until the man came and picked it up later on that day."

"So what are they planning on doing about replacing my car?"

"I checked into that for you, and I was told it would be around Christmas when they will have the one you liked replaced."

"Man, that's so messed up."

"What's the difference between having it now and Christmas?"

"I was hoping I could get them to send it to me before Christmas."

"Ben, it's just a car."

"No, it's just my car with all the customized bells and whistles that I wanted."

"I can't believe you got an attitude over a little car."

"Whatever. If it was something you wanted, and then it was gone, you'd be upset too. Forget that."

"If you say so, boo."

"Now my Christmas is going to be messed up."

"Why? Because you didn't get that silly little car? Boy, if you don't stop trippin."

"I'm not trippin'. That's the only thing I really wanted for Christmas." "What about your gift from me?" I asked him.

"The way you've been acting, I seriously doubted that you would get me anything." He said.

"The question is, did you deserve anything? You hadn't really been good, Ben."

He sighed. "Let's not get into that. I'm gonna go ahead and hang up now that we are talking again."

"Alright then, I'll talk to you later."

"Love you."

"Do you really?" I asked him.

"Is there a need to ask?"

"Do you really want me to answer that?"

"No. I will talk to you later. Bye."

Our call ended just when Phillip knocked at the door. We ordered room service, and talked about the cars he liked the best, and possibly considered buying. I kicked Phillip out around eight-thirty. I was so tired. I had to go to bed in order to be functional by the next day.

It was fifteen minutes after eleven when my phone started ringing. I reached over to answer without looking at the caller ID.

"Hello," I said in a whisper.

"Baby, you got to wake up."

"Ben?"

"Yeah, baby, it's me."

"What's wrong?"

"Nothing, baby. Stacey had the baby."

"Huh?"

"Stacey had the baby!"

"She did."

"Yeah. **He's an eight-pound, twelve-ounce, healthy, beautiful baby boy!**" He shouted.

"Well."

"Well, what?"

"Is he yours?"

"Baby, it's too soon. She just gave birth."

"I don't give a damn how soon it is. I want to know P. D. Q."

"P. D. Q.?" He asked.

"Yes, it means pretty damn quick."

"Can they rest first? We have plenty of time for that-"

"Well, I'm glad you think so, but I don't."

"I want to know his paternity as much as you do."

"You have a funny way of showing it."

"You act like I wanted to be in this situation."

"Maybe you should have thought about that before you cheated on me." He became quiet. "That's what I thought. Goodbye, Ben." I said, hanging up the phone.

He called right back.

"Tamara, don't do this to us. You said that you would forgive me, remember? You forgave me."

"That was before I knew what you had actually done. I will see you tomorrow."

"Don't hang up. Let's talk about this."

"I have to go before I say something that I can't take back."

"I don't want you to hang up with me being this angry."

"Ben, all we do is argue, and I'm tired. I'm tired of hurting. I'm tired of crying. I just can't take it anymore. Please, just let me hang up, and I will see you tomorrow, okay?"

"I love you, Tamara."

"That's very questionable. Bye."

I was so pissed off, I just hung up the phone. I didn't want to hear anymore. I got out of bed and took another shower. It wasn't my garden tub, but the hot water did the trick. I couldn't sleep, and I needed to talk. I called the only person I knew that would be awake this time of night.

Phillip.

Chapter 23

PHILLIP

Tamara called me right as I stepped out of the shower. She said she was feeling down and needed some company. I knew all too well what had occurred. She and Ben had yet another pow-wow. I toweled off and put on my silk pajama bottoms and slippers. Since our rooms were right next door to each other, I stepped out of my room and knocked on her door, figuring I wouldn't be there long.

Tamara answered the door, looking amazing. She was wearing a black satin nightie that left very little to the imagination. We stood there a minute, just eyeing each other up and down.

"Are you going to let me in, Ms. Lady, or what?" I asked.

By the look in her eyes, she wanted more than just to let me in.

"Um, I'm sorry." She said, stepping back so that I could come through. "You smell nice." She said, closing the door.

"Thanks." I smiled. "So, what's going on that has you down?" I asked sincerely, sitting on her bed.

"Ben. Who else?" She said, folding her arms and plopping next to me. "We got into another argument."

"Why?"

"Because his dumb ass refuses to get a DNA test."

"Huh?"

"He called to tell me that the baby had been born tonight. So, I asked him if they would perform the DNA test. He told me some stupid crap about letting them rest. Does he not understand how hard this has been for me?" She said, holding her head down.

"Tamara, you've waited this long. A week or so won't prolong the inevitable."

"Yeah, but ever since I'd tried telling Ben that baby wasn't his, he's been on a crusade to prove otherwise. It almost seems like he wants that baby to be his, which bothers me."

"I don't get it. I thought he wanted this to be over as soon as possible. What you are saying doesn't make sense."

"Well, apparently, he has you fooled, too."

"Nah, I know Ben better than that. He wants nothing to do with that girl." "Hmmph." She said, rolling her eyes.

"Tamara, I really don't know what else to say. I mean, I know you're upset by all of this, but I also know that Ben loves you and wouldn't do anything to hurt you on purpose." I said, rubbing her back.

"Well, why are you here and he is not?"

"You know that's not fair."

"What isn't fair is to have your life put on hold until someone decides to make up their damn mind about what they really want."

"What will you do if you know...it's true?"

"If it's his, I can honestly say that I'm outta there."

"You are going to give up everything you have with him because he made a mistake?"

"Phillip, if I go by how I'm feeling right now, it's already over."

"You don't mean that," I said, shaking my head at her.

"Yes, I do, just as I mean this." She said, leaning to kiss me.

"Tamara, what are you trying to do?" I asked, but I received my answer when our lips successfully connected.

I wanted Tamara more than anything, but I also knew she was reacting to the hurt she felt for Ben.

"Tamara, please," I whispered as I tried to withhold my desire to be with her. "Phillip, I need you." She said, looking me in my eyes.

"Tamara, you know...I-

That was all I could get out before we started back kissing. In my head, I knew we had come close before, but there was always something to prevent us from crossing the line. I couldn't help but wonder who or what was going to stop us now.

I just about had Tamara's nightie pulled over her head when her cell phone went off.

We looked at each other for a brief moment. I sighed.

"Answer the phone," I commanded her as if I was a jealous boyfriend.

"I don't want to."

"We both know who it is calling," I said, climbing out of her bed.

"Phillip, please don't leave."

"Go ahead and answer your phone, talk to your husband, and work it out. I'll see you later."

"I would rather continue what you and I had going on."

"Maybe, but all we could ever have is borrowed time."

"Why is it so hard for us to get together?"

"Who knows, but I'll see you later," I said, walking towards the door. "Phillip, wait." She said.

I turned around.

"Do you really have to leave? I mean, we were in the middle of something, and I really need your help to alleviate my stress, if you get my drift."

"In other words, all you want is to get back at Ben, and what better way to do that by sleeping with me, right?" I said, knowing it was the truth. "I am not, nor will I ever, be your pawn. If you really want a dose of reality, Tamara, this is the same type of game Stacey tried to play. Look at how well that turned out for her?"

After saying that, I left her room and returned to mine. I knew saying that to her was hurtful, but we can't go down this same path again. Even if we had slept together, I know she and Ben would soon make up, and where would that leave me? Nowhere. I've already resolved my issues with Kherington. I didn't intend to add any unnecessary drama to my life.

Chapter 24

TAMARA

It felt like my world was coming apart at the seams. Phillip left angrily. Ben keeps calling. I just don't know what to do anymore. To be with Phillip was going to be better than I had ever imagined. Then Ben had to call to ruin it. Phillip was right, though. I was only trying to forget about my problems with Ben. But to say I was playing the same type of games as Stacey was uncalled for. Phillip saying that to me was like being spat in the face. I wanted to run after him to explain that I was not using him, but I knew better. It was best to let things be. We should not have gone down that road to begin with. So why was I standing in front of his door like an idiot?

I knocked and turned my back to his door. When he answered, I turned around to face him and saw fire in his eyes. He pulled me toward him and kissed me passionately, and something went through me. I kissed him back with the same intensity. I needed to be with him.

"Phillip, please," I said, rubbing his face.

"Are you sure?" He asked desperately. "You know there's no turning back from here," he said, whispering in my ear.

"Yes, I know, but I need you," I replied, looking into his eyes. He kissed me again, leaving our clothes and inhibitions at the door.

Laying over me, he entered me slowly and deeply. My body quivered with each stroke. Tears ran down my face. It wasn't because of hurt or pain. My tears flowed because my body was being pleased, and it felt so damn good. I can't explain it. All I know is I've never experienced anything like this. He was so in tune with my body. He was giving me exactly what I needed and then some.

***

I didn't wake up until ten this morning, feeling so satisfied. Phillip was already up and dressed.

"Why didn't you wake me?" I asked him.

"Well, you looked so beautiful sleeping. I didn't want to disturb you."

"You could've awakened me. Now I have to rush to get ready to go."

"No, you don't," he said, standing on my side of the bed, leaning down to kiss me on the forehead. "You have plenty of time to eat the breakfast that I've ordered for you, and we don't check out until noon. So that will give you plenty of time to eat, shower, dress, and meet me at the airport."

"Meet you at the airport?" I asked, feeling some kind of way.

"Yeah, I have some business to take care of, plus I need to return that car outside."

"I forgot about the car. I thought you were going to purchase it?"

"I just might purchase something else. I'm not really sure about that one downstairs. It seemed more like your type of car than mine."

"That's true. So, what are you looking to get?"

"I'm still figuring that part out. I'm feeling that 2025 Tesla Roadster I drove." "That flashy red car?"

"Yes ma'am. I wouldn't have it any other way. I would slap some custom wheels on her, then place a personalized tag on the back, and show her off only on sunny, warm days with the top back. I think I'll name her Ruby."

"You and your friend," I said, shaking my head.

While thinking about that car, he stood there with the biggest Kool-Aid smile on his face.

"Your breakfast should be set-up in your room. Don't forget checkout is at noon." He said, finally coming out of his daydream.

"I won't. I guess I'll see you later." I said, putting on my robe while he was in the closet.

The elephant in the room was refusing to be ignored, but I had to. We kept the conversation light, being very careful not to say anything about last night. Phillip seemed different. It was as if he had become detached and was trying to put some distance between us. He picked up his carry-on, and I followed him out of the room. It was clear what the elephant in the room had become, guilt.

"Tamara...about last night," he said, turning to face me.

"There's nothing to talk about, Phillip," I said, trying to avoid the guilt that was slowly rising up.

"But we need to-

"No. I would rather us leave things where they are." I said, interrupting him. I walked past him and entered my room, closing the door behind me.

Just as Phillip said, my breakfast was waiting for me. He ordered me a bacon omelet with toast and juice. I ate my breakfast, took a quick shower, and dressed. I was holding my phone in my hand, thinking about calling Ben back, but I saw he had left a message, and I played it.

"Tamara, sweetheart, I am so sorry. I didn't mean for any of this to happen. I wanted to tell you what happened at our wedding rehearsal, but didn't want to hurt you. I knew you would be hurt no matter when you found out. I apologize for bringing this mess into our marriage. Tamara, I need you. I can't stand the thought of you hurting because of my stupid mistakes. Sweetheart, please don't leave me. I love you so much, please..." was all I heard of his message.

Guilt was eating me alive. I never considered the consequences or the repercussions. All I knew then was the pain I felt because of him. Now, he's pouring his heart out to me. Now, he was pleading for me not to leave him. What about then? Where was all this heart-felt emotion? Why is it on the eve that I've given up all hope of us ever rekindling what we once had that he reaches out?

He should be asking, was it too late? But was it too late? With all the damage done, can I ever wholeheartedly forgive him and move on? I'm more confused now than I was at the very beginning. I don't know where we're going to end up.

Chapter 25

BENJAMIN

I don't know what to do. I called Tamara back last night and basically put myself on the line. All I know is she is supposed to be back sometime today. She hasn't called or anything. I don't know what she's thinking or if she's even heard my message, for that matter. I know I messed up, but damn, how long is she going to hold this crap over my head? I was tired of waiting around the house until she decided to call. I asked TJ to meet me at Horizons. He was the only one I could really rely on. Phillip was gone, and Ce was somewhere acting all in love and stuff.

"Mr. Husband," TJ said, patting me on the back and sitting down with his Hennessy on the rocks. "What's good with ya?"

I guess my expression gave me away.

"Don't tell me it's trouble in paradise already." He said, adding in a little chuckle.

"That's exactly what I'm not going to tell you, but there is a problem." "Speak on it. I know you didn't call me down here to look at my pretty face, so what's up?"

"Man...Tamara. I called her last night to tell her that the baby had been born, and she wanted to know if I had the DNA test done."

"Well, did you?"

"Nah...man, Stacey had just given birth. What was I supposed to say, "Uh, after you clean him up, can you suave his cheek or take a sample of his blood so that I can prove paternity." I sighed and continued. "After Tamara basically hung up on my ass, to appease her, I asked Stacey if we could go ahead with the DNA test. Just as I thought, she got mad, blew up at me, and asked me to leave the hospital. So basically, here I am. My wife is mad at me, and there is no hope of a DNA test anytime soon. I know that if I wanted, I could have a court-ordered paternity test done, but I was hoping for something a little more civil."

"Civil my ass. Not with Stacey. You are going to have to get a court order. Especially if she's trying to hide the fact that the baby isn't yours. She'll prolong that mess as long as possible."

"I didn't tell you the best part. Before her blowing up at me, she wanted me to sign the birth certificate."

"Get the hell out of here. I know you lying!" He said then laughing.

"I wished I was, but it's the truth. She actually thought I was going to sign a birth certificate before I knew if he was mine or not."

"Well, let me ask you this. Did you see him...the baby, I mean?"

"Yeah, I saw him. He is so handsome, man. He's a shade or two darker than me, with curly black hair."

"Un-huh, but what color were his eyes?"

"Brown, I guess. I only got a chance to see him for a few minutes."

"Hell nah, man. That baby ain't yours." TJ said as he slapped his hand against the table.

I looked at TJ as if he was crazy.

"Do you care to explain to me how you would possibly know that?"

"Cause, if that baby's eyes are not partially hazel or green. He ain't yours."

"TJ, are you serious?"

"Hell yeah, I'm serious. Look at you and Ce, y'all get y'alls eye color from Pop. To think about it, everyone on Pop's side of the family has just about the same eye color. So if that baby's eyes ain't light and bright, she can kiss that check goodnight 'cause baby ain't yours."

"Well, thank you, Johnnie Cochran wanna-be," I said, laughing at that fool. "This coming from a man that couldn't get past biology without the help of some shortie."

"That is biology. All y'all got those light eyes, and that baby doesn't."

"It just so happened that genetically, Pop's eye color was more dominant than Ma's. But we could have easily come out with her eye color... which is brown."

"Whateva. I still say that baby ain't yours."

"I hope you are right, 'cause I don't know what's gonna happen with my marriage if it is."

"What I'll do is see what I can find out. Maybe Jasmine will tell me something."

"Do what you can. You know I appreciate any help I can get. Normally, Tamara and I would go around and around about this, but not this time, dawg. She stopped arguing. At least at the time I knew what she was thinking, but when they stop fighting back, it's only a matter of time."

"Yeah, man I know. I've been there before. That's when the call it quits.

"Man...mmm...mmm." He said, shaking his head.

What more could we say? I mean, Stacey had my back against a wall. This situation had me feeling low and so was my head until I heard her voice.

"Kherington," I said, straightening up in my chair.

"Hey. What are you all up to?" She asked.

"Nothin' much. It's been so long since we've seen you, girl. Where have you been hiding?" TJ asked while standing to hug her.

"Well, you know, your friend doesn't invite me to many of the gatherings anymore, so hey."

"So you mistreat me because he hadn't asked you to join us?" I asked, giving her a hug and a kiss on the cheek.

I always loved the way Kherington smiled.

"Ben, you know it's not like that."

"Un-huh, tell me anything."

"I hear congratulations are in order." She said.

"Yep, my boy here got married a couple of weeks ago. Maybe had you been there, he would have changed his mind and run off with you instead." TJ said, as if he was joking, but I knew TJ. He always wanted Kherington and me to hook up, and my marriage apparently didn't make much of a difference.

I shifted in my seat and cleared my throat.

"So what brings you to Horizons?" I asked her, changing the subject.

"Well, I thought I would catch your partner, but I see he isn't here." "Yeah, he's on a business trip and should be back sometime tonight."

"That figures? I was really hoping he would be here since it seems to be the crew's hangout spot. You might as well put your office over there in that corner."

"What's up with all of this, you all stuff? You are welcome here anytime. This is kinda like our extended office." I said joking. "Besides, we own the joint. So we may as well enjoy it."

"You're so silly. So he's in Dallas, huh?"

"Yeah, he and Tamara, my wife, are on their way back from Dallas as we speak," I said, hoping it was true. "So you may as well have a seat at our office that overlooks the dance floor. Isn't that right, TJ?"

"Sure is, and while you are at it, have one of our complimentary drinks on the house."

"Are you playing bartender too, TJ?"

"Hell nah, but I can go over there and ask Joe to make whatever it is that you like."

"Same ole TJ." She said, laughing. "I would like a glass of Merlot, please."

"Will there be anything else, your Highness?"

"No, TJ, that will be all for now. Thank you."

"As you wish, Madame." He said, bowing.

"I really miss you guys. Especially that clown over there." She said, pointing at TJ.

"Well, what do you expect to happen when you stop hanging around us?"

"You just don't understand, Ben. Phillip and I were having problems," she sighs, "and to make a long story short, we amicable agreed to end our relationship."

"I'm sorry to hear that."

"Not as sorry as I am to say it. We had been together, Ben, for a long time. What's so wrong with me that I wasn't good enough to be his wife?"

"Nothing as far as I can tell...but maybe you should be having this conversation with Phillip."

"No, really." She said, placing her hand on top of mine. "I value your opinion."

"Kherington, I-"

"Here you go?" TJ said, handing her the glass of wine she asked for.

"So you were saying?" She asked me.

"It was nothing. Have a drink or two with me, and we'll talk over old times. How does that sound?"

I was afraid I might have said something that I couldn't take back. Possibly the words that I should have said to her years ago.

"While y'all fraternize over old times. I'm gonna give y'all the deuces and head on out. Bye, Kherington, don't be a stranger." He said, hugging her.

"Watch it, man, don't be all up on my woman like that," I said, joking.

TJ and I slapped hands and bumped shoulders like we normally did. But this time, he held the embrace.

"Maybe you should've tried harder way back when and you wouldn't be reminiscing with your could have been." He said.

I pushed him back.

"Whateva, man. Bye." I responded.

It was good seeing Ben and Kherington together. I have nothing against Tamara, but it's just something about them two that I knew if they gave it a shot, it would stand the test of time. I just hated the pressure Ben was currently under. Stacey had just about messed up his marriage, and I knew her triflin' ass was going to hold up that DNA test. I'm just glad my situation with Jasmine had gotten better.

Heading home, I was wondering what I was gonna eat. Erica and I were in a weight loss competition together to see who could lose the most weight. She was gonna win this one 'cause I hadn't put down my alcohol long enough to drop a pound, much less weight. All this started when I told her she was looking a little thick in her jeans. Erica was a buck o five when she was wet. Her being a little thicker to me wasn't a bad thing, but she didn't take it that way. She was so beautiful to me. Erica was the perfect mixture of African and Filipino. Everything about her screamed Blasian, from her curves to her attitude. The only thing she inherited from her Asian mother was her almond eyes, long black hair, angelic face, and height.

Now she has me on this crazy ass diet. That's why I didn't eat at the club. I could've had the best well-seasoned porterhouse steak with all the trimmings, but it would have been my luck that I spilled some A1 sauce on my shirt. Ooh, that sounds so good with a loaded baked potato and a yeast roll. My mouth was just watering from the thought. I was getting ready to call Erica to ask her if I could have a cheat day just this one time when she called me.

"Hello."

"Hey baby, what are you doing?"

"Nothing thinking about you?" I told her.

"No, what are you doing for real?" she asked, laughing.

"That's what I'm doing. I was thinking about something to eat."

"You are so nasty, but I like it, though."

"You just like it, huh? You weren't saying that just the other night. But I was really thinking about something to eat for real, but I like your idea better."

"Your thinking is why you're in trouble right now."

"What kind of trouble am I in? I thought about the steak. I hadn't actually eaten it yet. You know I was gonna ask your opinion first...."

"TJ, before you start confessing, I have a question for you."

"Okay."

"What do you want, a girl or a boy?"

"Girl or boy?" I paused. "Are you telling me what I think you're telling me?"

"Yes, baby. We are pregnant!"

"Baby, are you serious?!"

"Yes!"

"When did you find out?"

"I found out minutes ago. I took a home pregnancy test."

"So, when do we go to the doctor?"

"We go on Monday, worry wart. I bet you were you this worrisome with JJ."

"Yes, I was. My baby is having a baby."

"Shut up. You are so funny. Sounding like one of those little old ladies."

"I'm so happy, baby," I said, laughing at myself. "This could not have happened at a better time. My second barbershop is up and running and doing well. What time is our appointment on Monday?"

"It's at ten o'clock."

"I can't wait until I tell my son he's going to be a big brother."

"I know his mother is going to appreciate that. He's already asking her a lot of questions. This is going to drive her batty for sure."

"What do I care? He's not asking me a lot of questions." I said, laughing. "You're so wrong. I bet if you had to be with him day in and day out, having him to ask you all kinds of questions, you would run away the first chance you got." "Well, that's his mother's fault, 'cause I told her know-it-all ass to put him in school. So if she wants to be batty, I say flap on sister."

"You know you're not right. I hope one day you get stuck with both kids for a week without any help."

"Uh-uh, y'all better come help me. Don't do that. Two babies and one man that ain't got a clue, don't mix." We laughed.

"Have some sympathy then. How long is it going to take before you get here?"

"Is now too soon?" I asked.

I looked at the mother of my child as if I saw her for the very first time. She was already glowing, more beautiful than I'd ever seen her before. We got what we both wanted. She got a chance to show me the pregnancy test as she jumped up and down. After making her stop, she fixed me a six-ounce sirloin steak and a baked potato with a little butter, a drop of sour cream, and with salt and pepper. It wasn't my porterhouse, and my baked potato wasn't loaded, but I did the best I could with my meal, not to forget my whole grain wheat roll. She still has me eating healthy, but she's the one getting ready to eat us out of house and home.

Chapter 27

TAMARA

We were having a party at Horizons with family and friends on Christmas Eve. Erica and I were at the buffet table more times than we cared to count. I told her I couldn't gain weight with her because she was pregnant. I also promised myself that I would exercise my butt off after the holidays. I liked being the perfect dime. Size included, but I could stand to tone up a bit. Just as long as my junk in the trunk wasn't flattening, my tah-tahs were still perky, and my thighs didn't jiggle like jello when I walked, it was all good. And even if they did, they made shapewear for that.

I couldn't wait for tomorrow. I wanted to know what Ben had bought me because I had something special for him. I hoped it would make this Christmas, the best Christmas he'd ever had. What can you give someone who could go out and buy whatever they wanted? Ben had only one of his gifts hidden at home, because I caught him snooping under the Christmas tree last week.

He and I had become friends again. When I returned home from Dallas, he met me at the airport. He held me as if I was going to fly away, and I felt his heart in that moment. It started when I listened to his voice message over and over again. He poured his heart out and I heard him. I decided at that moment to stand with him and not against him. After all, we were in this thing for better or worse.

As for Phillip and me, we remained cordial. Even though we crossed the line, I knew I could trust him to keep our secret. I hated to admit it, but he was right, and I regret involving him. I was so hellbent on hurting Ben that I lost a true friendship.

I was sitting with Erica at the table while she was feeding her face. I started watching Phillip and Kherington dance, and a flash from that night came back to me. If she got a portion of what I had, she was a lucky woman.

"What are you sitting over there grinning about?"

"Girl, looking at Phillip dancing with Kherington."

"They made a cute couple, don't you think? I wonder what happened."

"Who knows," I answered, looking dreamy-eyed. "It was nice of him to invite her to the party."

"Instead of you two gawking at someone else, would y'all like to dance," Ben asked, standing there with TJ.

"Come on, Erica, let's shake what our mamas gave us," I told her.

"Un-un girl, I can't do that." She replied.

"She sure can't," TJ chimed in.

"That's okay, 'cause I will shake it for the both of us."

Erica and I gave each other a high five.

Ben and I danced next to Phillip and Kherington. He was not as good with stepping as Phillip. And poor Kherington wasn't either. I wanted to glide over the dance floor, not box step. So, I decided to switch partners on the next song. All parties agreed, and it was on from there. Ben danced with Kherington, and Phillip and I owned the dance floor. To say we were showing out was an understatement. We danced for three straight songs-one sexy movement after another.

Phillip was rapping along with Jay-Z and pointing at me, talking about show me what you got. I showed him alright. They don't call it bounce music for nothing. When 'Back That Azz Up' came on, it was on. I think I dropped it like it was too hot because, after that, I needed to get a drink of water and find the nearest seat. I went back to our table to rejoin Erica.

"Tamara, what the hell? I thought I was going to have to run out there and hand you two a condom." She said, laughing, "Girl, how y'all were dancing was like you were auditioning to be on a BET: Uncut video."

"It wasn't that bad."

"Yes, it was girl. Even Kherington had to stop and stare. I should have hosed your butt down."

"Girl, please, I don't know what you are talking about. We were just dancing." I said, fanning and making eye contact with Ben, who didn't look too happy.

"If that's what you want to call it, girl. He might be your baby daddy after all of that bumping and grinding." She said, laughing. "Honey, if I didn't know any better, I would say you've been there before."

I just shook my head at Erica. She was too funny for words. I didn't say anything. I just maintained my smile as she was giving me the what's the tea look.

"Oh-oh, looks like somebody's in trouble," Erica said.

I looked in the direction she was talking about. There was definitely trouble in Horizons. Phillip and Kherington were in the corner going at it. She was pointing in my direction and fussing at him at the same time. Whatever she was saying, he didn't act too interested. I guess I was next because here comes Ben.

"Excuse me," I said, passing by Erica.

"Where are you going?" Ben asked with a frown and glowing eyes.

"If you must know, I'm going to the bathroom to touch up my make-up."

"That won't be necessary. We are leaving." He huffed.

"What do you mean we are leaving?"

"Just like I said." He barked.

I backed down. I didn't want to cause a scene. I grabbed my coat and told a few people goodnight.

We walked to his car, and he opened the passenger door. After I got in, he slammed the door behind me. Before he did that, I could already tell he was pissed off. Just by his jaw muscles flaring and biting on his bottom lip. Which looked sexy as hell, and oh my God, those eyes. I was so turned on by him being so angry that he wouldn't even understand.

"What are you looking at?" He asked.

"You wouldn't believe me if I told you."

"Try me." He said, glaring at me.

"What if I told you that you were super sexy right now, and all I want to do is..." I leaned over and whispered in his ear what I wanted to do to him and how I was going to do it.

He gave me a sexy smirk.

"So you think that's going to stop me from being angry with you."

"Uh-uh, I want you to keep that energy. I need that for something."

"Tamara, stop. I'm not playing," He said as I touched him. "Ooh...shi-. If I wreck my car...girl, I swear...ooh."

"Merry Christmas, baby," I said, waking her.

It was a quarter after seven in the morning. I had to wake her. I couldn't take it anymore. I was like a little kid when it came to Christmas.

"Merry Christmas to you, too. Why are you up so early? I thought after I put all that good lovin' on you last night, you'd be asleep till noon."

"Uh-uh, girl, it's Christmas! Baby, get up?" I said, pulling on her.

"Okay, okay. Can I at least go to the bathroom and brush my teeth? Dang." She said, getting out of bed and going into the bathroom.

"No, Grumpy Smurf. Just hurry it up in there."

"You just wait until I come out." She said.

It took her ten minutes to get out of there.

"Now, are you ready?" I asked.

"You sure are antsy to get nothing."

"I know you got something up in here for me."

"Have you been naughty or nice?" She asked.

"After last night, you tell me."

"Hmmm, let me think about that for a minute."

"Tamara!"

"What? Stop calling my name." She said, laughing.

"Stop playing."

"Alright, hold on. You look like you are about to cry."

"Ain't nobody crying. Tamara played too much. I really loved Christmas.

"Here, crybaby." She said, handing me a long flat box that was gift-wrapped.

I don't remember seeing this under the tree. I have to remind myself to check out her likely hiding places. I unwrapped the box and opened it. Inside there was an envelope.

"What's this?" I asked her.

"Open it. I'm dying to know what it says myself. It took all I had not to open this envelope before you did." She said.

I read the letter.

Dear Terrance Robinson,

This letter will answer any and all questions of

paternity. As it regards Cameron B. Harris, subject A

and Terrance Robinson, subject B. As it results,

ninety-nine point ninety percent out of

one hundred percent proves that you.........

STAY TUNED AS THE DRAMA CONTINUES...

A Thin Line Between Regret & Redemption

COMING SOON!

How did you like the book?

Share your thoughts with me at ddmiles.author@gmail.com.

Want to Read More?

Feel free to visit me on the web at www.relationshipreflections.org.

www.ingramcontent.com/pod-product-compliance
Lightning Source LLC
Chambersburg PA
CBHW070653010826

48975CB00013B/1100